Clara in t

Copyright © 2016 by S Cartlidge
All rights reserved. This book or any portion thereof
may not be reproduced or used in any manner whatsoever
without the express written permission of the publisher
except for the use of brief quotations in a book review.

This is a work of fiction. Names, characters, places and incidents either are products of the author's imagination or are used fictitiously. Any resemblance to actual events or locales or persons, living or dead, is entirely coincidental.

For my mum.
First my mother. Forever my friend.

Chapter 1

What am I doing? I must be crazy. I must have *completely* lost my mind. Rubbing my throbbing temples, I bounce Noah on my hip and flash the airport assistant a strained smile. A nine-hour flight with four babies, three immature adults and one very stressed out husband is *not* my idea of fun. Looking around the crowded airport, I try to remember why we are doing this. Just think of the beach, I tell myself. Just think of the sea breeze and the blissful feeling of warm sand beneath your feet...

'No!' Gina yells, snatching a passport out of Madison's tiny hands. 'How many times have I told you not to do that?'

Obviously not happy at being told *not* to rip the pages out of her passport, Madison throws herself onto the floor and lets out an almighty scream. Lord, give me strength. We haven't even checked-in and already I want to turn back and go home. You can probably tell from the chaos that this trip wasn't planned all that well. To be honest, it wasn't planned at all. In fact, it was only last week that our neighbours invited us to their villa in Barbados for a week of sunshine and cocktails. With Noah being so young, I was a little dubious about taking him on a long-haul flight, but I have to admit that I had a hidden agenda.

You see, my best friend, Lianna, has been having somewhat of a long-distance relationship with a man she met whilst on a working holiday to the island last year. It sounds lovely, doesn't it? Perpetual single woman finds love on the idyllic island of Barbados. It's like the perfect little love story. Although if you know Lianna's dating history as well as I do, you will be aware of why I am more than a little dubious over the whole affair. From numerous failed engagements to holiday romances gone wrong, Lianna really has been dealt a rough hand in the dating department. I have lost count of the number of times I have heard her declare that she has found *The One*, only for it all to end in tears a matter of weeks later. Therefore, when Owen and Eve offered us the opportunity to join them at their villa for a week, we jumped at the chance of meeting Li's mystery man.

When I say *we,* I don't just mean myself, Oliver and Noah, the Strokers decided to come along, too. With Owen and Eve having a villa big enough to house the five thousand, it was pretty much a no-brainer. For those of you who don't know, the Strokers are some of our closest friends and as of last year, our new neighbours. Until a couple of years ago, Marc was my manager at Suave, a major shoe label in the fashion industry, which is coincidentally where I met Lianna. The three of us bonded over a love for Rioja and chicken kebabs and it wasn't long before we became inseparable. Like all good things, our time at Suave came to an end and we all went our separate ways, sort of. Marc took his wife Gina and made the leap down under, Lianna set up her own interior design company, Periwinkle and I decided to move to the suburbs and start a family with my Texan husband, Oliver.

Needless to say, it turned out the suburban lifestyle wasn't for us and it wasn't long before we returned to bustling London. No matter how hard I tried to adjust to the rural way of life, the buzz of the city was something that I just couldn't leave behind. Surprisingly, Marc felt the same way and he returned to the UK a year after he left for Australia. In true Stroker style, they came back with a bump (literally) and baby Melrose was born a few months later. Melrose makes up the final member of the Stroker family, joining her older siblings, Madison and Marc Junior. Gina wasted no time in revealing that Melrose was named after the hotel where she was conceived. That baby girl doesn't know how lucky she is that she wasn't fertilized a few weeks earlier when they were staying at The Kooky Koala.

'You're next to me.' Lianna smiles happily and hands me a boarding pass, snapping me out of my daydream. 'I asked them to put the Strokers on the row behind.'

Looking over my shoulder at Madison who is *still* screaming hysterically, I breathe a sigh of relief and follow her through the airport. 'Have you heard from Eve?' I ask, dodging an irate couple who are arguing over their lost luggage.

'I have.' Lianna nods in response and flicks her long, blonde hair over her shoulder. 'She called this morning. Honestly, she is *so* excited to see us.'

Smiling in response, a frisson of excitement washes over me. If you would have told me a year ago that Eve and Owen Lake would have become such a big part of our lives, I never would have believed you. There was actually a time when I thought Eve was a home-wrecking prostitute, but we don't talk about that anymore. It's one of those stories that you lock away in the back of your mind and try to erase from existence.

If you are not already aware, the Lakes used to be our neighbours when we moved to the suburban village of Spring Oak. After dealing with more drama than the residents of Wisteria Lane, they decided that the suburbs weren't for them either and they purchased the city centre apartment below ours. It's true that a stupid case of Chinese whispers almost cost us our friendship, but things are now better than ever and since we moved back to the city our relationship with the Lakes has been rock solid.

'I can't wait for you to meet Vernon.' Lianna sighs, her eyes sparkling brightly.

'Mmm...' Struggling with Noah as he fights to get down, I exhale loudly and shake my head in annoyance.

For the past few weeks, all he has wanted to do is walk. Well, *try* to walk. Since he turned one, he has been determined to do things for himself. Even feeding time has become an epic battle as he tries (and fails) to use a spoon independently, resulting in a pureed potato catastrophe in the kitchen.

'He is just... *perfect*.' Lianna whispers, emptying the contents of her cosmetic box into a clear plastic bag. 'I mean it this time. I have finally found *The One*.'

Resisting the urge to point out that I have heard her say those same words at least ten times in the past, I scoop up Noah as we approach airport security. Oblivious to my ignorance, Li continues to wax lyrical about the new man in her life.

Hearing a commotion behind me, I spin around to see a flustered trio in the form of Marc, Gina and Oliver. With each one carrying a different bawling child, they really do look comical. A smile spreads across my face as I watch Oliver attempt to make MJ laugh by turning him upside down and tickling his tummy. Letting out an ear-piercing squeal, MJ laughs hysterically before reverting back to full-blown brat mode.

Not wanting to get dragged into the pandemonium, I hand Noah to Lianna and walk through the scanner. Thankfully, I managed to dodge the dreaded red light and proceed to collect my hand luggage from the conveyor belt. As I wait for the rest of our group to join us, I fiddle with my watch and laugh as Noah tugs on Lianna's hair. Since we moved back to London, Noah and Lianna have become the best of friends. Seriously, his little face lights up the second that he hears her voice. I wish I could say the same, but I have actually started to get a little worried about her lately.

You see, Lianna has a habit of falling too hard, too fast and given that she has only ever spent a mere seven days with Vernon, I am right to be concerned that history is repeating itself all over again. In the way that only Lianna can, she has spent the last ten months Skype calling, Snapchatting and not that I want to think about it, but *sexting*. Obviously, I want her to be happy, I just don't want Li to get her feelings trampled on, again. Let's face it, on paper Vernon Clarke does seem too good to be true.

Born in Florida to Bajan parents, Vernon decided to make the move back to his homeland five years ago. Apparently, giving up his bank job to open up a beach bar in Barbados was the best thing he ever did. Vernon's new business venture, The Hangout, is a laidback beach bar on a secluded part of the exclusive west coast. Frequented by locals and celebrities alike, it's very easy to see why Li has fallen head over heels, not just for Vernon, but for Barbados as well. I should know, Lianna has bent my ear about it for so long now I feel like I have already been.

Hearing the body scanners buzz loudly, I look up to see Gina being led away by a rather hunky male security officer. The man in question is causing quite a stir amongst the women in the queue and they're not being very discreet in their admiration for him. Spotting a watch hanging out of her back pocket, I wave my arms around to get her attention. It wouldn't surprise me if she has left that in there on purpose.

Catching her eye, she flashes me a wink as a devilish smile plays on her lips. Taking Noah from Lianna, I try to stifle a giggle as Mr Dreamboat points to a row of waiting women. Obviously remembering that men aren't allowed to body check women, Gina's face falls as a busty, butch body inspector pulls on a pair of gloves and motions for her to follow her. Lianna clutches my arm as we burst into hysterics simultaneously. Well, I guess that backfired...

* * *

Looking out of the window, I shoot the air stewardess an apologetic smile as Noah sobs uncontrollably. Bless him. He has done so well. We are seven hours into the flight and he has slept for six of those. Looking over my shoulder, I am astounded to see that the Strokers are sound asleep. Taking up the entire middle row, Marc and his family are drooling away into their headrests. Even baby Melrose is enjoying forty winks as she snuggles happily into Gina's arms.

In spite of myself, I can't help but feel envious. I have never been able to sleep on a plane. No matter how tired I am or how many glasses of fizz I drink, I am constantly aware that we are thirty thousand feet in the air and might plummet to our deaths at any given moment. Dramatic, I know.

'Two hours to go!' Lianna whispers, her voice filled with hope. 'One hundred and twenty minutes. Seven thousand two hundred seconds...'

'Alright!' I laugh, passing her Noah. 'I get it...'

'Are *you* excited, Noah?' She asks, holding him up so that he can see out of the window. 'Your first time abroad! We're going to build sandcastles and swim with the turtles. You are going to love it.'

Taking advantage of having my hands free, I snatch the drinks menu from the seat pocket in front of me and wonder if I can squeeze in another glass of wine before we land. Deciding that I can just about manage it, I press the buzzer and wait for the stewardess. It has been so very long since I last left the UK that I had almost forgotten just how much I have missed being in sunny climes. Don't get me wrong, I love London. No, I *adore* London, but the feeling of sunshine on your skin is one that you just cannot put a price on. That incredible sensation of the salty sea breeze in your hair as you lay back and soak up those delicious rays.

A smile plays on the corners of my mouth as a frisson of adrenaline bubbles in the pit of my stomach. Something tells me that this holiday isn't going to be your typical sun, sea and sand escape...

Chapter 2

'Has everyone got their bags?' I yell above the commotion in the airport. 'Yes? No?'

'I think we're good.' Marc mumbles, grabbing MJ and throwing him onto his shoulders. 'Which way is the exit?'

Not having a clue how to get out of the building, we decide to follow the crowd and weave through the sea of buzzing people. Despite Lianna insisting that she knew *exactly* where she was going, she succeeded only in leading us to multiple dead ends. After such an early start, we are all beyond exhausted. Well, when I say *we*, I mean the adults. The children seem to have woken up full of the joys of spring and I am yet to decide whether or not that is a good thing.

'I want to go to the beach!' Madison squeals, running ahead through the airport. 'Beach! Beach! Beach!'

Locking eyes with Gina, I try not to laugh as Madison proceeds to ask a tour guide for directions to the beach. She really does have an unbelievable amount of confidence for a four-year-old. The elderly tour guide lets out a chuckle and hands Madison a balloon painted with the flag of Barbados. Thanking her for the kind gesture, Gina takes hold of Madison's hand as Lianna marches on ahead.

'Have we booked a mini-bus?' I ask Marc as we approach the exit. 'I don't even know where we're going, do you?'

Shaking his head in response, Marc hands me MJ in exchange for my suitcase. 'Eve booked the transfer.'

Leaving the men to deal with the transport, I hang back with Gina and the children.

'My God, it is hot in here!' Gina moans, tearing off her jeans to reveal a pair of pink hot pants.

'Gina!' I whisper angrily. 'What are you *doing?*'

'What?' She retorts, folding up her jeans and stuffing them into her handbag.

Did she really travel in two layers of clothes? Shaking my head in disbelief, I take out my map and attempt to fan my face. Her usually glossy black hair is stuck to her face and the once perfect foundation is now streaming down her full cheeks. As ridiculous as she looks stripping off in the airport, I can't help but wish that I had done the same. To say that I am melting in my skin-tight leggings and trainers is an understatement.

Peeling off Noah's cardigan, I tie my own jacket around my waist and check my watch. Due to the time difference, it is still only early afternoon, meaning that we have plenty of time to get settled in at the villa before the sun goes down.

'Is it too early for a rum punch?' Gina asks, eyeing up a passer-by's drink mournfully.

Seemingly overhearing our conversation, the drink holder spins around and points to his cup. 'You're in Barbados! It's *never* too early for rum...'

'I think you got your answer!' I laugh, waving off the friendly holiday-maker and picking up Noah.

'I think I did...' Gina gasps, taking off her sunglasses for a better look at the hunky gentleman.

'Oi!' I giggle, slapping her on the arm. 'Marc's right outside.'

'A bit of window shopping never hurt *anyone*.' She winks wickedly before bursting into a fit of giggles.

'What are you shopping for, Mummy?' Madison asks, tugging off her shoes and throwing them onto the floor.

Fighting the urge to laugh, I raise my hand in acknowledgement as Oliver appears in the window and beckons us outside.

'I think the car must be here.' I yawn loudly and attempt to gather the children together.

With Noah on one hip and MJ on the other, I leave Gina to get the girls and make my way outside. As soon as we step out of the building the heat from the sun washes over me. Popping on my sunglasses, I breathe in the fresh air and take in my surroundings.

The sky is a stunning shade of blue, with pristine white clouds expertly scattered along the horizon. Huge palm trees line the roadside, giving you a glimpse of what lies ahead. A tingle of excitement runs through me as I enjoy the sensation of the warm sun on my skin. Suddenly the long-haul flight seems totally worth it. I would fly for an entire week if it meant I would arrive here at the other end.

Spotting Marc waving his arms above his head, I clutch the boys tightly and motion for Gina to follow suit.

'Where's the transfer?' I ask, looking around in confusion.

Following Marc's gaze, I turn around to see a giant pink Hummer parking behind a fleet of taxis. He can't be serious!

'Don't you just love Eve?' He laughs loudly and proceeds to carry our cases over to the waiting vehicle.

Eve! Of course! A hot pink hummer is not so strange now that I know Eve is behind it. Wiping a bead of sweat from my forehead, I follow Marc and Oliver across the road. The sun is high in the sky, giving out a glorious warmth that is unmistakably Caribbean sunshine.

Feeling the skin on my neck start to tingle, I suddenly worry that the children should be wearing sun cream. Handing Noah and MJ to Oliver, I rifle through my suitcase for my Piz Buin. Successfully locating a bottle in a mountain of bikinis, I line up the kids and give them a good dousing of the white paste before buckling them into their seats.

'Is this bubbly?' Gina squeals, clapping her hands together excitedly as she pulls open a tiny fridge to reveal numerous bottles of very expensive fizz.

'This is Eve that we're talking about!' Lianna laughs loudly as she climbs into her seat. 'Of *course*, it's bubbly!'

Accepting a frosty glass of fizz, I pull a funny face at Noah as the driver turns on the radio and pulls out onto the open road. Relaxing reggae music floats out of the speakers as we speed along, causing Madison to throw a little party in her car seat. Thankfully, the air-conditioning kicks in immediately and I breathe a sigh of relief. I cannot wait to get out of these sticky clothes. Flying in a pair of leggings is suddenly seeming like a pretty stupid idea. Glancing over at Gina, who is relaxing in her shorts and flip-flops, I give in and kick off my trainers.

Lianna's phone pings loudly and she immediately snatches her handbag to retrieve the handset. Jabbing frantically at the screen, a ridiculous smile spreads across her face as reads the text. You can practically see love hearts floating around her head.

'Is that *the boy?*' Gina teases, draping her legs over Marc's knee.

Li nods coyly and leans back in her seat. Oh, Lord. I have seen that infatuated look before and it never ends well. Keeping my opinions to myself, I flash her a smile and concentrate on my fizz. Palm trees whizz past the windows as I close my eyes and allow myself to savour the moment. It has been so long since I had a foreign holiday and I intend to enjoy every bloody second. Seven heavenly days of Bajan bliss lie ahead, and I couldn't be more thrilled about it if I tried...

Chapter 3

'Omg...' I mumble, my eyes widening as I try to take in my surroundings.

From the second the hummer came to a stop outside a set of huge electric gates, I have literally been jaw dropped. Seriously, my jaw has been hanging open for the last seven or eight minutes.

'Well? What do you think?' Eve asks, taking Noah from my arms for a cuddle.

Not knowing what to say, I hold up my hands feeling totally lost for words. Apart from the fact that it had eight bedrooms, I actually didn't know anything at all about Eve's villa before we left the UK. Although looking around this place, I think it's safe to say that nothing could have prepared me for this. Situated on a beautifully secluded lane, Dovedale House takes up a bigger plot than most football pitches. The grand pillars that greet you at the entrance are just a hint of the luxury that awaits you inside. From incredible chandeliers that glisten like diamonds to the magnificent marble flooring that runs through the entire property, it's clear for anyone to see that not a penny has been spared. I have to hand it to her, Lianna really did do a fantastic job on the refurbishment.

'It's unbelievable.' I manage at last. 'Thank you so much for inviting us.'

Eve plays down my gratitude and leads the way outside. Following behind like a doting puppy, I resist the urge to squeal and raise my eyebrows at Gina. I can tell by the look on her face that she is equally as impressed. I mean, how could you not be? The huge open space and astonishingly high ceilings make you feel tiny in comparison and the fact that you can actually hear the ocean is just the icing on the cake. Grabbing Lianna by the arm, I pull her to one side and allow the others to continue on the tour.

'Li!' I squeal. 'You never said that it was like this!'

'What do you mean?' She whispers, adjusting a stunning painting on the wall that is slightly off centre.

'You know what I mean!' My voice is a few decibels higher than I intend, but I can't contain my enthusiasm. 'This place is incredible!'

It really is spectacular. The colossal kitchen, the spiral staircase, the fabulous fixtures and fittings... I feel like I have died and gone to Barbados heaven.

'You haven't seen anything yet.' Lianna's eyes sparkle as she grabs my hand and drags me through the house.

Struggling to keep up with her, I almost trip over my own two feet as we tear through the living area. Coming to a stop at a set of huge glass doors, Li spins around to face me.

'Close your eyes!' She pulls the voile curtains closed ensuring that I can't see what is outside.

'What?' I laugh, batting her hands away. 'Why?'

'Just do it!' Li demands, covering my eyes with her hands.

Not having any choice, I allow her to momentarily blind me. The last time I allowed her to blindfold me we ended up knee-deep in mud being chased by a herd of sheep, but that's another story altogether.

'Ready?' She asks, swinging open the doors and pulling me outside.

The sun shines down on my skin as we take a few steps forward before she whips away her hands, leaving me completely speechless. The beach! We are practically two strides away from the sea! The most beautiful, azure water that I have ever seen laps against the powder white sand, enticing you in with its gentle waves. Shielding my eyes from the powerful rays of the sun, I let out a gasp as I realise that the rest of our group have wasted no time in getting acquainted with their new surroundings.

Tearing off their t-shirts, Owen and Oliver splash each other playfully as they run into the ocean. Obviously not wanting to wet her hair, Gina is sitting under a parasol along with the children. If I could design my own little version of heaven, this is it.

'Come on.' Lianna giggles, kicking off her shoes and running across the sand.
'I'll race you.'

Watching her sprint into the waves, squealing loudly as she goes, I burst into laughter and follow her lead. Tossing her sunglasses onto the sand, she pushes Owen into the water before hiding behind Oliver for safety. Looking around, I realise that we are on our own secluded section of the beach. Glistening water stretches out as far as the eye can see, making you feel totally marooned in paradise. Removing my socks, I peel off my leggings and stride into the ocean. The warm waves lap against my legs and my entire body tingles from head to toe. This is out of this world. How much does a place like this cost? Five million? Ten? Just thinking about numbers that big makes my head hurt.

As Lianna wraps her arms around my shoulders, a huge wave knocks us both off our feet. Laughing hysterically, we attempt to get up before deciding to stay right where we are. The water washes over our bodies as we float on our backs, staring up at the beautiful blue sky ahead. This is paradise. It really, really is. A pelican swoops down into the water, causing Lianna to scream wildly and the rest of the group to burst into hysterics. Taking in the picture-perfect scene, I find myself thinking, if this did cost ten million pounds it was worth every single penny...

* * *

Draping my legs across Oliver's lap, I clink my glass against his and breathe in the salty sea breeze. I must be on my third delicious glass of rum punch and each one tastes better than the last. After our impromptu dip in the ocean earlier, Eve instructed her chef (yes, *chef*) to whip us up some dinner. Unbelievably, James produced a stunning three-course meal that wouldn't look out of place at any high-end restaurant. Just thinking about the fabulous flying fish and scrumptious salt bread makes my mouth water uncontrollably. Who knew that bread could taste *so* good?

Chewing on the end of my straw like a hungry beaver, I pull my beach towel tightly around my body and look out at the black water. Apart from the laughter coming from our group, the entire beach has fallen into a dark silence. Enjoying the sensation of the sea breeze on my skin, I look down at my rosy shins. Just a couple of hours of fun in the sun has left my pale English skin tinted a rather embarrassing shade of pink. No surprise there. I knew I should have had a quick dousing of St. Tropez before we left the UK.

Eyeing up Lianna's golden glow enviously, I excuse myself to check on the children. Even though the sun went down hours ago, the tiles are still warm under my feet as I walk along the veranda and into the villa. Slipping into one of the downstairs bedrooms, I use the screen of my phone for light and poke my head into the cot. Bless him. Noah is totally wiped after such a long day and is snoozing away happily with his arms above his head, just like his daddy does.

Quickly snapping a photo on my phone, I peek into the other two cots at MJ and Melrose before covering Madison with a blanket. Four sleeping angels. There really isn't anything more beautiful in the entire world than sleeping children. Checking that the baby monitor is working correctly, I make my way back outside and stretch out on a lounger.

'What are we talking about?' I ask, reaching down for my glass.

'Lianna's boyfriend.' Gina whispers, flashing me a wink.

'Oh...' I shoot Lianna a smile and scratch my ankle. Damn mosquitoes. 'When do we get to meet the infamous Vernon?'

Smiling coyly, Li twists a strand of blonde hair around her finger and sighs dramatically. 'Soon...'

'Soon?' Gina yells. 'When is soon? Tomorrow? The next day? When?'

'Give the girl a break.' Eve laughs, throwing an arm around Lianna's shoulders.

'That's easy for you to say.' Gina scoffs. 'You've already met him!'

Suddenly remembering that it was Eve who introduced Li to Vernon, I roll onto my side and get ready for the interrogation.

'I have...' Eve teases, flashing Lianna a wink. 'And I am pleased to say that he is just lovely.'

Gina squeals loudly and claps her hands together. 'I need *all* the details.'

Sensing that they are in for a whole lot of girl talk, Owen, Oliver and Marc excuse themselves and escape to the games room, leaving us four women alone.

'Well...' Eve kicks off her sandals and smacks her lips together. 'Owen and I met Vernon Clarke a few years ago when we hired The Hangout for Owen's birthday. He is such a genuine man. He really, really is.'

Lianna nods in agreement and digs out her mobile. 'I know you have already seen it, but this is him.'

Gina takes the handset and squints at the screen. 'Wow!' She mouths, before holding up the screen for me to see. 'Very nice.'

Having been subjected to hundreds of images of the handsome Vernon over the past twelve months, I am extremely aware of exactly what he looks like. Don't get me wrong, being insanely tall, with muscles bigger than Wladimir Klitschko and flawless black skin, he isn't exactly bad to look at, but it's going to take a little more than a muscular body to convince me that he is the man for Lianna.

'What makes you so sure that he is *The One?*' Gina purrs, leaning down and running her fingers through the sand.

Pretending not to listen, I walk along the veranda and enjoy the sound of crickets chirping happily. We haven't even been here for twenty-four hours and already I can feel the stresses of the daily grind melting away. As much as I love summertime in England, nothing can compare to the tropical climate of the Caribbean.

'Well?' Gina presses, as Lianna sighs heavily.

'I don't know...' Li breathes. 'I really don't.' Eve and Gina exchange confused glances as Lianna stares at a photo of Vernon on her phone. 'Although I do know that I want him today, tomorrow, and every day for the rest of my life.'

'Awwh!' Eve whispers, holding a napkin under her eyes as Gina smiles widely. 'You two are made for each other. I can just feel it.'

Glancing over my shoulder at a sentimental Lianna, I find myself hoping that Vernon feels the same way. She really has been hit with a serious case of the love bug. Listening to her gush about finding the perfect man, I wouldn't be surprised if she floats right out of her seat. My mother always told me that the higher you fly, the harder you fall, and I really don't want to be the one to catch her if this all goes belly up.

A round of applause drifts out from the villa and Eve decides that's her cue to go and see what the boys are doing. As Lianna and Gina follow her inside, I take a moment to enjoy a few deep breaths of the warm fresh air. There's something about being on a tropical island that makes you fall in love with life again. It makes you realise that perhaps life isn't about avoiding risks, maybe it's about finding out what it is that makes you truly happy and not stopping until you get it...

Chapter 4

Peeling open my eyes, it takes me a moment to realise that I am not in my own bed and another thirty seconds to remember that I am not even in my own country. It's safe to say that the enormous four-poster bed that Oliver and I have been snoozing in is a little different to our bed back home. Stretching out my legs, I roll over to see the sun shining brightly through the open window. Not wanting to disturb Oliver, I slip out of bed and wander across the room.

The gentle rustling of palm trees entices me out onto the balcony as Noah starts to stir in his cot. Plucking him up, I plant a kiss on his nose before walking over to the huge double doors. Lifting the sheer curtain, I throw open the doors and smile widely as the warmth of the morning sun washes over me.

Taking a seat on a plush quilted lounger, I position Noah in the shade and look out to sea. The shimmering rays of sunlight dance on the crisp blue water, creating a sparkling display as far as the eye can see. From my position on the balcony, I can see a few early birds setting up under a palm tree. Obviously not wanting to miss a second of the beautiful morning sun, they strategically lay down their towels before smothering one another in tanning oil. Ouch, I think to myself. That is going to hurt tomorrow. Just like any holiday destination, the beach starts to fill up quickly. Feeling thankful that we have our own secluded section of the beach to play on, I scoop up Noah and head back inside.

Leaving the door open so that the unmistakable sound of waves crashing against the shore drifts into the room, I drop down onto the bed and give Oliver a gentle nudge. Placing Noah onto Oliver's stomach, I stifle a laugh as he crawls up to Oliver's head and tugs on his hair playfully.

'I think Noah is telling you that it's time to get up.' I whisper, pushing myself to my feet.

Stretching his mouth into a lazy smile, Oliver takes Noah and blows a raspberry on his stomach. As usual, Noah bursts into a fit of giggles and squeals like a piglet at feeding time. After kissing both of them on the nose, I twist my hair up into a messy ballerina bun and slip into the bathroom. I didn't really see much of the en-suite last night, as by the time that we crawled into bed it was almost 2am. Pushing open the heavy wooden door, I let out a gasp as I take in the exquisite marble wet room.

'Wow...' I breathe, running a finger along the sleek black tiles.

This is my idea of heaven. Anyone who knows me is aware of just how much I love a soak in the tub, and this isn't just any old bathroom. The chandelier that hangs proudly in the centre of the room sparkles like crazy as the sunlight bounces off the delicate crystal. Resisting the urge to touch it, I grab a towel from the rack and walk over to the shower. The shower, if you can call it that, is made from the most beautiful stained glass and could easily hold five or six people. I have never seen anything quite like it in my life.

Not having a clue how to turn the damn thing on, I resort to jabbing idly until a powerful stream of water floods out of the enormous shower head. Letting out a squeal as it pounds into my back, I tip my head back and allow the warm water to wash over my face. Gentle reggae music seeps into the bathroom from the open window and I dance around in the shower happily. The sun is shining, Bob Marley is playing and there's a rum punch on that beach with my name written all over it. I think it's safe to say that today is going to be a good day...

* * *

'What the hell is that thing?' Lianna giggles, digging out her phone to snap a photo of Gina and her frankly ridiculous hat.

'It's fabulous and you know it.' Gina fires back, smothering Melrose in sun cream. 'Fashion is not meant to be understood by everyone.'

'Oh, please.' Li scoffs. 'Carrie Bradshaw, you most certainly are not.'

Handing Melrose to Marc, Gina takes the bottle of cream and chases Lianna around the veranda. Watching the two of them scream like a pair of schoolgirls, I check my beach bag for all the essentials. Not that it really matters if we forget anything, we are only two strides from the ocean after all.

'How was breakfast?' Eve asks, stepping outside in a stunning pink kaftan. 'I hope James looked after you?'

'It was delicious.' I gush, licking my lips as I think back to our frankly amazing breakfast. 'James is a superstar. I think I have fallen a little bit in love with him.'

Let's face it, how could you not fall in love with a hot Bajan man who makes you Eggs Benedict whilst you sip on a cold glass of bubbles? Eve chuckles and pulls on her Givenchy sunglasses. With Eve attending a yoga class down on the beach every morning, she wasn't around to enjoy breakfast with us. For a fleeting moment, I did think of joining her, but doing a downward facing dog in thirty-degree heat isn't my idea of a relaxing holiday activity.

Hearing a flapping sound behind me, I spin around to see Oliver and Owen dressed head to toe in snorkel gear.

'Well, I guess you two have got plans for today.' I look down at their giant flippers and laugh loudly.

'We most certainly have.' Owen confirms happily, tying his underwater camera to his wrist. 'Fancy joining us, Marc?'

Taking a sip from my bottle of water, I try to hide my smile. I already know what his answer is going to be.

'I think I'll sit this one out.' He forces a yawn and scoops up Madison who is tearing around on the sand in her princess armbands.

'You sure?' Owen asks. 'There's some incredible fish right here in the bay.'

Shaking his head in response, Marc grabs Gina's beach bag and strolls across the sand. Catching Gina's eye, I apply a thick layer of cream to Oliver's back before waving him and Owen off on their underwater adventure. Watching them stroll towards the ocean, I smile proudly and snap a photo of them on my phone.

Poor Marc. It's no secret between his closest friends that Marc can't swim. I first discovered this on an impromptu visit to Spain many years ago. Whilst Lianna and I spent an afternoon diving into the infinity pool, Marc stayed firmly glued to his lounger. It took him a good couple of years to admit that he has a fear of water. Apparently, an unfortunate lilo malfunction is to blame for this irrational anxiety over getting his hair wet. No matter how much encouragement Li and I have given him over the years, nothing at all has tempted him to try and face his fears.

Popping a pair of baby sunglasses on Noah, I hold him on my hip and follow Gina and Melrose down to the water. The breeze blows my hair gently as we walk, providing great relief from the sweltering heat. Looking over my shoulder for Lianna, I smile as I realise that she has stopped to build a spontaneous sandcastle with MJ. With her hair in a rustic fishtail braid and a quirky cut-out swimming costume, she looks like a different person to the Lianna of late.

Since she set up her interior design firm, Periwinkle, Li has been more than a little stressed out, although I can completely understand why. Being the managing director of a successful business *is* going to take its toll. With conferences in Paris, working lunches in Madrid and a list of high-profile celebrity clients to deal with, it's easy to see why she doesn't have any time left for herself. I have tried and failed to encourage her to take some days off, but all she seems to do is work. Seeing her now without the obligatory power suit and tablet glued to her hand, she looks like the carefree Lianna that I once knew and loved.

Setting out one of Eve's plush beach towels on a sunbed, I strategically pull the playpen into the shade. The beach playpen is one of the most genius inventions in the world. The canvas sides and hooded top ensure that babies can enjoy the beach without getting into any trouble. Happy that he has enough sun cream on, I take Melrose from Gina and sit her beside him. Bless them. They are ridiculously cute when they're together. Gina and I joke that they will get married in the future, but if Melrose turns out to be anything like Gina, my little Noah may run in the other direction.

At less than two years old, Noah already has a defined personality. Just like his father, he is independent, easy going and absolutely gorgeous. Melrose, on the other hand, is equally as gorgeous, but she is already a diva in the making.

Stepping out of my purple maxi dress, I pluck a magazine from my bag and breathe a sigh of relief. This is the life. I could most certainly get used to this. Trying not to look as Gina whips off her hot pants and adjusts her neon green string bikini, my mouth stretches into a smile as Eve appears behind us with a tray of drinks.

'Anyone for a refreshment?' She trills, holding out a luscious cocktail. I look down at my wrist for the time, only to discover that I left my watch in the room. 'Go on then.' Well, it would be rude not to, wouldn't it?

Taking a sip of the creamy coconut concoction, I nod appreciatively and flash Eve the thumbs-up sign. That tastes *so* good and *so* bad at the same time. If I have many more of these, I think there's a good chance that my clothes aren't going to fit by the end of the week. Obviously not having the same body worries, Gina drains her glass in one before reaching for another.

'You might want to go easy on those.' Eve laughs. 'They're deceivingly strong.'

Gina shakes her head defiantly and chews on the end of her straw. Being completely used to Gina's stubborn behaviour, Eve rolls her eyes and peels off her kaftan to reveal a flawless gym-honed body. With her platinum blonde hair and rock-hard abs, she is really the perfect beach bum. Sucking in my mummy tummy, I take a sip of my cocktail and try not to feel envious. Between skinny Eve and curvy Gina, I feel like the piggy in the middle.

Whilst Eve puts a lot of blood, sweat and tears into looking good, Gina is one of those infuriating women who eats pizza morning, noon and night, yet has womanly curves in all the right places. To be honest, Gina must be a good couple of stones heavier than I am, but whereas my weight gravitates to my stomach, hers seems to avoid the area completely. The enormous breasts and butt that rivals Kim Kardashian just seem to get bigger with each pound that she gains. Annoyingly, her stomach stays bizarrely flat, despite her not lifting a finger to exercise in years.

Telling myself not to feel self-conscious next to my two gorgeous friends, I take a deep breath and enjoy the sensation of the warm air washing over my body. Listening to Gina and Eve discussing their plans for the week ahead, I find myself starting to relax. After all the chaos of the past twelve months, this holiday is well overdue. Between moving back to the city from Spring Oak and helping Marc and Gina with baby Melrose, things have been hectic, to say the least. For months now I have been pestering Oliver to whisk me away for some fun in the sun. I have lost count of the number of times I have dreamed of Spanish siestas and gorgeous Greek beaches. Not once did I expect to be rushing off to Barbados like Inspector bloody Gadget.

'Fancy a dip?' Lianna's voice springs me from my daydream. 'I'm going to take MJ for a paddle.'

'I want to paddle, too!' Not missing a beat, Madison jumps out of Marc's arms and tears across the sand.

Pushing myself to my feet, I leave Gina to watch Noah and Melrose and take hold of Madison's sticky hands. Unsurprisingly, Madison insisted on applying her own sun cream and is now a sticky ball of white paste and sand. Watching her waddle along in her Minnie Mouse swimsuit, I let out a giggle as she swings her arms back and forth. The water washes over our toes and she squeals in delight. Bending down to pick up a handful of sand, she discovers a tiny pink shell and plonks down in the water to inspect it. Sitting down beside her, I grab a handful of sand and give my legs a quick exfoliation.

In the distance, I can see two pairs of flippers bobbing about in the ocean and I am pretty sure that one of them belongs to my husband. Holding onto Madison tightly as the strong waves push us further up the beach, I smile as Li dangles MJ's legs into the water. Even though it's easily thirty degrees, the ocean spray makes the humidity bearable. It's hard to believe that this same blue sky is grey and overcast back home. Not wanting to think about the daily grind that we left behind, I grab Madison's bucket and start to make a sandcastle.

As usual, Little Miss Independent takes charge and gets to work at digging up the sand. Not wanting to miss out, MJ breaks free from Li and starts to help his big sister. Taking the opportunity to talk to Lianna, I wait for her to sit down next to me before I speak.

'Well, you were right.' I sigh, running my fingers through my tangled curls. 'Barbados really is paradise.'

'I knew you would love it.' Stretching out her long limbs, she takes down her straps to avoid the dreaded tan lines. 'But you haven't seen anything yet. I have so much planned for this week. Catamaran trips, the famous fish fry, rum tastings and of course, The Hangout.'

My stomach flips at the mention of The Hangout. Since we arrived here, we haven't really spoken much about Vernon, which is strange because for the past twelve months it is all she has talked about.

'The Hangout...' I repeat, watching her cheeks flush pink. 'When is that scheduled for?' She picks up a handful of sand and lets it run through her fingers, obviously avoiding my question. 'Well?' I probe, not wanting to drop the subject so easily.

'We can go whenever you want.' She replies casually, shrugging her shoulders as if she isn't really bothered.

'How about right now?' I fire back, determined to get a date out of her.

Li laughs loudly and shakes her head.

'Tonight then?' I pester, shielding my eyes so that I can see her face.

Looking up at the sky, she taps her foot and smiles. 'How about tomorrow?'

I nod in response as Madison puts the final handful of sand into the bucket and instructs Lianna to flip it over. Tapping the bottom of the bucket, she lifts it up to reveal a perfect castle.

'Yay!' MJ squeals, clapping his hands furiously and running over to Marc to show off his handiwork.

Not wanting to let MJ have all the credit for her sandcastle, Madison tears off after him.

Feeling the sun on the back of my neck, I let down my hair and allow the waves to pull me into the water. The last thing I want to do is burn and ruin the rest of the trip. Slipping my sunglasses onto my head, I spot Eve waving from the veranda. Catching my eye, she points to my empty cocktail glass and I flash her the thumbs-up sign. Warm sun, turquoise waters and rum cocktails – what more could you ever want?

Dipping my shoulders under the surface of the water, I swim out until my feet no longer reach the sea floor. Hundreds of tiny fish dart between my legs as I kick to stay afloat. Flashes of yellow, orange and silver twinkle in front of my eyes, creating a dazzling display of colour. Regretting not bringing my underwater camera, I tip my head back and let my hair soak through. The buoyancy of the water makes me feel completely weightless as I float on my back. I could stay in here forever.

Making my way back over to Lianna, I hold out my hand to pull her to her feet. The sun is now high in the sky and even though he is in the shade, my mummy instincts are telling me to give Noah another coat of sun cream. I have only been in the sun for an hour and my shoulders are already pink. What I would give to get a golden glow like Li.

Trudging up the sand, I pull over a parasol and pluck Noah from his playpen. In his dolphin-print shorts with matching t-shirt and hat, he looks ridiculously cute. Digging around in my bag, I take out his water bottle and try to get him settled. I was a little worried about how he would handle the heat, but he seems happier than usual. Batting away my hands he attempts to hold the bottle himself, resulting in water trickling down his t-shirt. Not wanting a screaming match, I leave him to it and reach down for my magazine, only to realise that it isn't where I left it. There's only one magazine thief around here and they answer to the name of –

'Gina!' I snatch the mag out of her hands and playfully hit her with it. 'I haven't even read that yet.'

Sticking out her tongue, she rolls off her lounger and sashays over to the playpen, twerking along to the music as she goes. Spotting their mum jump around like a crazed monkey, Madison and MJ erupt into a fit of giggles. Their little faces crease into laughter as they collapse onto the sand. Unable to resist joining in with the hysterics, I shake my head and chuckle quietly. There's always one and thankfully for me, it's *always* Gina...

Chapter 5

'Seriously, Clara. You have absolutely *no* idea how amazing these fish are.'

Nodding in response, I roll my eyes and tug on a swimming costume. Ever since Oliver returned from his snorkelling trip yesterday, he has not stopped raving about what lies beneath. From the friendly turtles to the vibrant reefs and shoals of playful fish, I must have seen over a hundred images in the last hour alone.

'Look at this.' Handing me the camera, he smiles broadly as I flick through the images. Images that I have looked at ten times already.

'That's fantastic.' I stretch my lips into a smile and try not to get agitated.

Now, you might be thinking that I could have a little more patience with my excitable hubby, but the truth is that today I have bigger fish to fry. After much pestering on my behalf, Lianna finally agreed to let Gina and I visit The Hangout and I have just five more minutes to find an outfit. Don't ask me why it matters to me so much what I wear to meet Li's boyfriend as I don't know myself, but I do know that I have tried on everything in my suitcase and nothing feels quite right.

Settling on a flamingo print sundress and a pair of leather gladiator sandals, I twist my curls into a messy top knot and sigh loudly. This will have to do. After all, it's too bloody hot to wear any of the maxi dresses that I brought, and all my playsuits just stick to my thunder thighs like pigs in a blanket. With a quick slick of lip balm, I grab my sunglasses and check my handbag for all the essentials. Unlike all my holidays prior to having Noah, my essentials now include some not so glamorous items. From spare nappies to Sudocrem and cleansing wipes, the days where my handbag contained nothing more than my phone, keys and a Chanel lipstick are long gone.

After a final glance in the mirror and a quick spritz of bug spray, I turn my attention to Noah. Snuggled into Oliver's chest, he seems perfectly content nibbling away at his fingers. I almost don't want to disturb him, but Oliver and Owen have another day of underwater activities planned so Noah is coming with me. Thankfully he will have a playmate to keep him occupied as Gina and Melrose are tagging along, too. Lianna wasn't too pleased about that part. Gina is a handful at the best of times, so I'm not surprised that she is a little apprehensive at the prospect of introducing her to the new man in her life.

Scooping up Noah, I plant a kiss on his soft cheek before strapping him into his pram. A quick glance at my watch tells me that it's almost time to leave. With The Hangout being a little further than walking distance away, Li thought it would be best to hire a car rather than traipsing the children through the hot morning sun. Feeling a little miffed at having to leave before breakfast, I try to ignore the rumbling that is coming from my stomach.

'Alright, you have fun today.' I lean down and kiss Oliver goodbye, resisting the urge to climb back under the sheets with him.

'You, too. Call me if you need me.' Stretching out his brown arms above his head, he yawns lazily and grabs a pair of shorts from the floor. 'Hey, do you know if Marc wants to join us today?'

Not wanting to embarrass Marc by revealing his secret, I shake my head and make for the door. 'I think Marc has daddy duties today.' Smiling regrettably, I blow him a kiss and grab my handbag. 'I shall see you later. Love you.'

Enjoying the cool air-conditioning on my sunburnt skin, I flash Gina a smile as she stumbles out of her room. Wearing a sheer crochet dress with Melrose strapped to her chest in a bright yellow baby carrier, she doesn't exactly look restaurant appropriate.

'I'm not changing.' She retorts, as though reading my mind.

Holding my hands up to surrender, I pop my sunglasses onto my head and lead the way through to the kitchen. Just like yesterday morning, James is hard at work preparing another delicious breakfast. My nostrils flare like a hungry hippo as I take a seat at the kitchen island.

'Good morning, James.' I smile broadly and accept a piece of fruit from the bowl in front of me. 'How are you today?'

'Good morning!' Sprinkling a handful of spinach into a frying pan, he whistles along to the music and tosses a tea towel over his shoulder. 'Can I get you some breakfast?'

I am about to ask him if he can whip up a cheeky omelette when a car horn beeps loudly outside. 'That will be Lianna. Thanks anyway, James.'

Taking Noah's pram, I say a quick goodbye to Eve and motion for Gina to follow me outside. When Li left an hour ago to collect the car, she didn't explain that by *car,* she meant huge red Range Rover. Rolling down the window, she slides her sunglasses down her nose and raises her eyebrows mischievously.

'You like?' She smirks, turning up the radio so that reggae music floods out of the speakers.

I open my mouth to respond, but Gina beats me to it. 'I *love* it!' She squeals, clapping her hands together excitedly and throwing open the passenger door.

Looks like I'm in the back with the babies then. Impressed to discover that she has remembered to get car seats, I whip Noah out of his pram and buckle him in safely. Collapsing the pram in one swift movement, I toss it into the boot and dive in beside him. According to Li, The Hangout is situated on a secluded corner bay further down the same beach, so it shouldn't take us too long to get there. Waiting for Gina to stop dancing and fasten Melrose into her seat, I fan myself with my handbag and will her to hurry up. Can't she see that I'm melting back here?

Slamming the car door shut, she bangs on the dashboard and instructs Lianna to drive. As she speeds along the rustic road, I poke my head into the front of the car and eye up Lianna's outfit. Considering that she has talked about this meeting for almost a year, she doesn't exactly look dressed for the occasion. In a pair of tiny denim shorts and a loose-fitting white vest top, she looks like one of the hippy students you see at Camden Market. Catching her eye in the rear-view mirror, I stick out my tongue and flash her a wink. Her usually poker-straight hair is tousled from the humidity and her freckles are on full view for the world to see. She hasn't even got any makeup on! To anyone else, the fact that Lianna has left her skin bare might not mean much, but I know that Lianna doesn't reveal her freckles for just any old man.

Looking out of the window as the world rushes by, I start to feel a little nervous about what we are about to do. What if I don't like him? Do I tell her? Do I keep it to myself? Hearing her laugh with Gina, a pang of hope washes over me. From commitment-phobes to serial cheaters, Li seems to be a magnet for the wrong men. After all of the useless relationships Lianna has been in over the years, isn't it about time that she found Mr Right?

Last night after dinner when the rest of the house had retired to bed, Marc and I spent a good hour or so discussing Lianna's old flames. The most unfortunate thing with Li is that she has never put a foot wrong in any of her relationships. I would even go as far as to say that she is pretty much perfect when it comes to her behaviour with the opposite sex. The only thing she is guilty of is giving someone her heart without taking theirs in return. I just hope that this time will be different.

Pulling over onto the side of the road, Li flicks off the car engine and spins around to face me.

'We're here.' Her face is alight with anticipation as she unbuckles her seat belt and dives out onto the road.

Looking around dubiously, my brow creases into a frown as I take in my surroundings. This can't be right. Sliding out of the car, I shield my eyes from the sun and shoot Gina a quizzical look. We appear to be in an abandoned car park that is surrounded by huge leafy trees. Tipping her head upside down and giving her hair a quick scrunch, Li shoves her keys into her back pocket and proceeds to get Melrose out of the car. Totally puzzled, I follow suit and unbuckle Noah.

'Do I need the pram?' I ask, trying not to show how perplexed I am.

'Nope. You won't need your shoes either in a moment...' She smiles brightly and points through the trees. 'It's this way.'

Locking eyes with Gina, I shrug my shoulders and follow Lianna through the thick branches. A leaf falls onto Noah's head and he giggles happily. I am about to ask her where the hell we are going when I suddenly get a glimpse of turquoise blue ahead. Squinting my eyes, I let out a gasp as we reach the end of the wooded area and stumble out onto soft white sand. Letting out a surprised laugh, I slip off my flip-flops and pop them into my handbag. Li was right, we really won't need our shoes.

Unlike the section of beach down at the villa, this is rugged and unspoilt with natural imperfections that somehow make it more perfect. Strangely, the water in the bay is almost completely still, making a great contrast to the roaring waves back at the villa. Stopping to commit the scene to memory, I look out to sea and run my toes through the white sand. The sun bounces off the water, almost blinding me with the light. Watching Lianna saunter off ahead, I adjust Noah's hat and strategically walk under the row of swaying palm trees. We approach a slightly rocky patch of sand and pause for a moment to watch a tiny crab hurriedly making his way back to the ocean. As Lianna snaps a photo of Gina and the crab, I continue walking ahead and discover that the bay curves to the right.

Letting curiosity get the better of me, I wander along the sand until I can see around the corner. The sea breeze blows my hair into my face as I do a little jog, desperate to get a glimpse of The Hangout before Lianna realises that I am missing. Panting for breath, I lean against a palm tree as I spot the all-important building. There it is. The Hangout. Made entirely from wood with a straw roof, it's not at all what I was expecting. Unable to control myself, I walk further for a closer look. Hammocks hang from the palm trees that line the entrance, tempting you to jump in and relax. Tucking a stray strand of hair behind my ear, I am about to investigate further when I hear footsteps coming from inside.

Dammit! Quickly turning on my heel I attempt to run back to the others, which isn't as easy as it sounds when you are holding a chubby toddler.

'Hey!' A deep American voice hollers behind me. 'Can I help you?'

Damn it.

Chapter 6

Suddenly frozen to the spot, I bite my lip in panic and slowly spin around. I know from the thousands of photographs I have seen that this tall muscle machine in front of me is Vernon. Seeming to lose the ability to speak, I open and close my mouth repeatedly like a hungry goldfish.

'Vern!' Lianna squeals loudly, running past me and jumping into his huge arms.

Even with her ridiculously long legs, she looks like a tiny child in comparison to Vernon. Her statuesque frame is dwarfed by his huge physique, which is a first for Lianna. I shield my eyes from the sun and try to weigh him up. He's bloody gorgeous, I know that much. With big brown eyes and a smile that would outshine any Hollywood superstar, it's impossible to say he is anything less than perfect in the looks department. Showering him with kisses, Lianna seems to have forgotten that Gina and I are standing behind her. Finally tearing herself away, she jumps down onto the sand and entwines her hand with his.

'This is Vernon.' She declares, struggling to get her breath back.

'Well, I got that.' Gina cackles, rocking a sleeping Melrose in her baby sling.

'You must be Gina.' Vernon lets out a low laugh and holds out a hand. 'Vernon Clarke, it's a pleasure to meet you.'

Gina bats his hand away and leans in for a kiss on the cheek. Rolling my eyes, I offer my hand and give it a firm shake. It will take more than a dreamy body and a seductive accent to win me over.

'I'm Clara and this is my son, Noah.' I shoot him a thin smile and point to Noah. 'It's great to finally put a face to the name. I've heard a lot about you.'

'Likewise.' Bending down, he holds out his hands to Noah, who unbelievably leans over to let him pick him up. 'How's it going little buddy?'

Staring at my son open-mouthed, I feel genuinely shell-shocked. Noah is so fussy about who he will go to; I cannot believe that he is giggling away with a complete stranger. Lianna stares at Vernon like she is going to burst with pride. I must admit, it is unusual to see a man be so comfortable around children when he doesn't have kids of his own. Most guys run a mile at the mere mention of babies.

'Can I get you ladies a drink?' Vernon smiles widely and throws his free arm around Lianna's shoulders. 'Something to eat, maybe?'

I am determined to keep a clear head today so cocktails are off the menu, but my rumbling stomach would *not* be happy if I turned down the offer of breakfast.

'I could eat.' I return his smile as we walk across the sand towards The Hangout.

Lianna and Vernon walk a couple of strides ahead with Noah and I take the opportunity to get a moment with Gina.

'Well?' I whisper, holding my wild hair out of my face. 'What do you think?'

'I think he's hot!' She exhales dramatically and I hit her on the arm. '*Gina!* I'm being serious!'

'Serious about what?' Li calls over her shoulder.

My cheeks flush pink and I stammer over my words. 'We were just saying that we are seriously hungry.'

She squints her eyes at me suspiciously as we step over the threshold. Thousands of twinkling lights surround the entrance, adding a touch of glitz to the driftwood sign that hangs overhead. Simple, yet so successful in creating an air of elegance to the modest building. Taking off my sunglasses for a better look, I blink for my eyes to adjust them to the dark and scan the room. Wow! This place is seriously cool. The sand from the beach carries on inside and a funky chalkboard advises you that shoes aren't compulsory. Following Lianna's lead, I take a seat at the bar and look out over the water. I bet you get incredible views of the sunset from here. The way that she raved about this place I expected something much grander, but I totally understand what she means about it having an air of prestige. With luxury VIP booths and glossy champagne menus on every table, I can completely appreciate why it is frequented by celebrities wanting to escape their hectic lifestyles.

Taking Noah from Vernon, I sit him on my lap and flash Lianna a wink. Bless her. She has been staring at me with bated breath for the past five minutes. I know that she is waiting for me to give her my opinion on whether Vernon passes the Clara test or not, but I haven't made my mind up just yet. Yes, Noah bizarrely seems to have fallen in love with him and Gina was drooling the second that she laid eyes on him, but the jury is still out for me.

'Wait there. I have someone that I would like you to meet.' Vernon bangs his hand on the bar and disappears into the back.

Lianna's brow creases in confusion as she watches him walk away. I am about to ask her what's going on when he returns with a rather beautiful woman.

'This is Stephanie, my new bar manager.' He smiles proudly and takes a step back.

'Hi, Stephanie!' We say in unison, stretching our mouths into Joker-worthy smiles.

'It's a pleasure to meet you all.' Stephanie bows her head and grins back. 'Welcome to Barbados.'

'You finally found someone then!' Lianna laughs, holding out her hand for a shake.

'I did.' He laughs quietly and places a hand on Stephanie's shoulder. 'It wasn't easy, but Stephanie is exactly what I was looking for.'

Stephanie smiles proudly and gives Vernon a wink. Wearing a sleek black trouser suit and a shiny new name badge she certainly looks the part. Taking in her pretty face, I immediately develop a bit of a girl crush. Her perfectly symmetrical features are framed with a mass of glossy curls, curls that I could only ever dream of achieving with my frizzy mane. She's definitely a good face for the business, that's for sure.

'Vernon tells me that you're all hungry? I'm going to get the chef to make you a traditional Bajan breakfast.' With a flash of her pearly whites, she strokes Noah's head before making her way into the kitchen.

For a moment, we sit in silence until we can be sure that she is out of earshot.

'I like her.' Lianna whispers, nodding in approval. 'I like her a lot.'

'She's great.' He confirms, sliding onto a stool. 'We're lucky to have her. Now, what can I get you to drink?'

Gina picks up a champagne menu and I roll my eyes. Any excuse for a glass of fizz. I don't think I've ever seen her turn down the offer of bubbles, ever.

'I'll just have a sparkling water, please.' Noah starts to grumble, and I stand up to let him toddle around.

'You *have* to let Vernon make you a rum punch!' Lianna squeals. 'They are so good.'

'Maybe after breakfast.' I giggle, chasing after Noah.

'I'll have one.' Gina pipes up, not missing a beat.

'Alright.' Vernon laughs, jumping over the bar. 'One sparkling water and a rum punch.'

'Make that two rum punches.' Lianna smiles, twirling a strand of hair around her finger like a love-struck teenager.

'You can't have one, you're driving!' I give her my best *mum* look and shake my head.

Sticking out her tongue, she jumps to her feet and readjusts her shorts. 'Come on, I'll give you the tour.'

Grabbing Noah before he can swallow a handful of sand, I hold him on my hip and follow Li back outside. Obviously not wanting to leave the bar, Gina stays put and waves us off. Shielding my eyes from the sun, I listen intently as Li runs through a typical day at The Hangout.

'So, this is where we have the fish fry.' She points to a patch of sand and I look at her dubiously. 'It doesn't look like much, but people come from all over the island on fish night.'

'Really?' I ask, not convinced.

'*Really.*' She repeats seriously. 'And it's not just locals, the press are *always* sniffing around to get a glimpse of the VIP clients.'

'That's amazing.' I concede, unable to hide how impressed I am. 'Did you see anyone famous when you were here?'

'Unfortunately not, but just last week Vernon sent me photos of Brad and Ang! They hired the entire place just for the two of them!' Her eyes sparkle and I completely understand why.

'Wow!' *Brad and Ang!* I think I would pass out if I saw Brad and Ang. 'Amazing! Where's next on the tour?'

'Well...' She looks around and bites her lip. 'The hammocks here are where the customers watch the sunset, but you have to get here early or you won't get one.'

Taking Noah from me, she climbs into a hammock and rocks it gently, laughing as he squeals with delight.

'So...' She takes a deep breath and looks down at the sand. 'What do you think?'

I try to perch on the hammock next to her and jump up when it nearly capsizes.

'I like him, and you seem to certainly like him.'

'I don't just like him, Clara. I *love* him.'

Pursing my lips together, I resist the urge to tell her that I can't understand how you can love someone after just seven days.

'I know what you're thinking. How can I love someone after just seven days? But it isn't just seven days. Vern and I have talked on the phone every day for the past year.' I look her in the eye and keep my opinions to myself. 'We have spoken about everything from marriage to children. This is it, I know it.'

'Marriage? How would that even work?' I ask, kicking myself as her face falls in disappointment.

'We would *make* it work.' Her voice is small, and I can tell that I have hurt her feelings.

Forcing myself to smile encouragingly, I spin around as Vernon appears on the decking and waves us over.

'I think our drinks are ready.' I grab Noah and hold out my hand to help her up. 'We had better get in there before Gina gets her grubby paws on them.'

I hold Noah on my hip as we make our way back inside in complete silence. I feel bad about not being more positive, but it just seems so far-fetched. Is Lianna going to move to Barbados? Is Vernon going to move to London? Neither option is feasible, so I really don't understand how she thinks this is going to pan out. Holding out my hand for hers I give it a friendly squeeze as we take our seats at the bar.

'How's the rum punch?' I ask Gina, who is slurping away at her cocktail happily.

'Fabulous.' She holds out the glass, but the stench of alcohol on her breath is enough to make me decline.

Unlike Noah, Melrose has been snoozing since we got here. Snuggled into her baby sling, she is completely oblivious to her surroundings. Gina doesn't know how lucky she is that all three of her children can sleep through a category five hurricane. I wish I could say the same for Noah. Unfortunately he has the ability to hear a penny drop from three rooms away.

Flashing Stephanie a smile as she breezes past with cutlery and glasses, I pass Noah over to Lianna.

'If you would like to retire to the booth, ladies. Your breakfast is coming.' She winks cheekily and rubs her hands together.

Licking my lips as my stomach rumbles loudly, I slide into the plush booth and take a sip of my water. How people leave the house without breakfast in the morning is *beyond* me. As Gina tears herself away from the bar and its tempting drinks menu, I peek at Vernon and Li from behind my glass. You would never believe that they have spent just seven measly days together prior to this. It's amazing to think that they are so comfortable around each other. They certainly look loved up, that's for sure. Anyone would think that they were newlyweds from the way that they are carrying on. The little voice in the back of my mind reminds me that love and lust are two very different things, I just hope that she isn't confusing the two.

Gina slides in next to me and unties Melrose's baby sling before expertly transforming it into a mini sleeping bag. Placing the sleeping baby in the booth opposite, she strokes her head gently and smiles before collapsing into her seat. I am about to quiz her about Vernon when Stephanie reappears with steaming plates of food. My mouth stretches into a smile as she places bowls and platters onto the wooden table.

'OK...' Stephanie claps her hands together and smiles. 'We have flying fish, eggs, onions, peppers and plantain. Enjoy.'

I eye up my plate greedily and pick up a fork. As usual, Noah demands to be fed first and I chop up a piece of fish before inspecting it for bones. Expecting him to spit it straight back out, I am surprised when he screws up his hands into little fists and shrieks with delight.

'Oh, you like Bajan food?' Stephanie laughs loudly and strokes his chin. 'This one can come again.'

Thanking her for the food, I lock eyes with Lianna and beckon her over. If she doesn't put Vernon down soon her food is going to go cold.

'How is it?' Vernon asks, picking up a piece of fish and tossing it into his mouth.

'Fantastic.' Gina swoons, digging in like she hasn't had a decent meal in months. 'The best food I've have had since we arrived. Just don't tell James!'

'James?' Vernon asks, throwing an arm around Lianna's neck. 'Who's James?'

'The chef back at the villa.' Li explains, still not touching her food. 'He's very good, but not as good as Patricia.'

'I will be sure to let Pat know that.' He laughs and motions for Lianna to sit down. 'Sit. Eat.'

She looks up at him with eyes like saucers and immediately dives into her meal.

'Aren't *you* eating?' I ask, realising that he hasn't got a place setting.

Shaking his head in response, he grabs a stool and sits down. Thankfully, Lianna takes control of the conversation meaning that I can concentrate on enjoying my food. Feeding pieces of fish to Noah, I listen intently as Vernon fills Lianna in on just how hard it was to secure his new bar manager. Apparently, for the past five years Stephanie has worked for a rival restaurant further down the beach. After many, many terrible interviews with prospective candidates, Vernon decided that he would try and tempt Stephanie with a huge pay rise. Ethical? Probably not. But I guess desperate times call for desperate measures.

Suddenly deciding that he doesn't want to eat anymore, Noah lets out a screech and kicks his little legs in protest. Resting him on my lap, I attempt to quieten him down as to not disturb the others.

'Let me take him.' Vernon stands up and holds out a hand for Noah. 'Wanna go see the ocean?'

Staring at him in silence, Noah considers his options for a moment before lifting his arms in the air for Vernon to pick him up. Watching the two of them walk away, I smile fondly and return to what's left of my meal.

'Isn't he just great with kids?' Li sighs dramatically and plucks a piece of coconut bread from the bowl in front of her.

'Does he have any of his own?' Gina asks, taking a slurp of her drink and leaning back in her seat.

'No.' Lianna shakes her head. 'He was married before, but children just never happened for him.'

My ears prick up at the mention of him being married before, she has kept that one quiet. Not wanting to be judgemental, I dab my mouth with a napkin and push away my plate.

'When are you going to introduce him to the others?' I probe, very aware that they will be back at any moment and I might not get another chance to ask.

'Possibly tomorrow. Owen and Eve already love him, so just Marc and Oliver to win over now.' She chews on the end of something that looks like a banana and smiles. 'That's presuming that he gets your seal of approval?' She looks between myself and Gina, her smile momentarily frozen.

'I think he's great.' Gina smirks. 'I really do. Handsome, friendly, great with kids... what's not to like?'

Turning her attention to me, I feel her eyes burning into the side of my head. 'Clara?'

I pause for a moment and look out to sea, carefully choosing my words before I open my mouth. Hearing Noah laugh as Vernon tosses him up into the air, I already know my answer.

'Well... I guess he's alright.'

Lianna squeals loudly and claps her hands together. 'Really?'

'Really.' I shrug my shoulders and flash her a wink. 'Besides, if he is willing to put up with you, he can't be all that bad...'

Chapter 7

Putting a freshly bathed Noah down for a sleep, I rub some moisturiser into my pink shoulders and slip on a simple maxi dress. With Oliver in the shower, I have a good thirty minutes to get myself ready before dinner will be served. After our yummy breakfast earlier, I didn't think that I could eat another bite, but a few hours of sunbathing at The Hangout has given me quite the appetite. Stretching out on the bed, I crank up the air-conditioning and take the opportunity to close my eyes for a moment.

Now that I have met Vernon, I feel like a huge weight has been lifted from my shoulders. All that stress and worrying about him being bad for Lianna has melted away. I don't think I have ever met a person before who is as genuine and sincere as Vernon Clarke.

Hearing the lock on the bathroom door click open, I roll onto my side and smile as Oliver steps into the bedroom. His crisp white shirt makes his tan look ten shades darker than it did this morning and his floppy chocolate curls hang loosely around his face. Watching him fasten his watch and run his fingers through his hair in a poor attempt to style it I let out a little laugh.

'Here, let me do it.' Taking a tub of wax from the dressing table, I place a dollop into my hands and set to work at fixing my hubby's crazy curls.

Unlike my own wild mane, Oliver's hair seems to fall perfectly no matter how long or how dishevelled it gets. Standing back to admire my handiwork, I nod in approval and plant a kiss on his cheek.

'Perfect.'

'Thank you.' He raises his eyebrows mischievously and perches on the end of the bed. 'So, how did it go with Vernon?'

When we arrived back from The Hangout earlier, Oliver and Owen were still out at sea, so we haven't had the chance to talk about it.

'He's fab.' I shrug my shoulders and scratch my nose. 'I wasn't expecting him to be, you know that, but he really is fantastic. He's super friendly, Noah loved him, and he seems totally besotted with Li.'

'That's great!' He rubs my arm encouragingly and reaches for his shoes. 'I told you it would be OK.'

I roll my eyes and wander over to the cot to check on Noah. I have to hand it to Oliver, he wasn't at all worried about Vernon. He seemed to think that if he wasn't serious about Lianna he would have lost interest long before now. Stroking Noah's cheek, I pull the blanket over his legs and grab my handbag.

'All that fun in the sun must have tired him out. I've never seen him sleep so soundly.'

Oliver pokes his head into the cot and smiles fondly. 'Looks like the Barbados lifestyle suits him.'

I nod in agreement and lead Oliver onto the balcony. We have been here for three days now and we haven't had more than thirty minutes alone together. Well, not without one of us snoring anyway. The water glistens under the moonlight, casting a shimmering strip of light across the sea. Wrapping my arms around his waist, I rest my head on his chest and breathe in his familiar aftershave. The Caribbean might be spectacular, but my favourite place in the world to be is right by Oliver's side, wherever that may be.

Laughter drifts up from the veranda below and I pop my head over to see Owen and Eve giggling happily. They really are a fantastic couple. Of all of our friends, they really are the most unlikely twosome, but they couldn't be more perfect for each other if they tried. Spotting us staring, Eve raises her glass and motions for us to come down.

'Be there in a minute.' I whisper, not wanting to wake Noah. Spinning around to face Oliver, I tuck a stray curl behind my ear. 'I think they're ready for us.'

Letting out a yawn, Oliver shakes his head in a bid to wake up. It seems that Noah isn't the only one who could do with an early night. Smoothing down my dress, I slip back inside and check on Noah for a final time before we make our way down to the dining room.

The delicious smell of chilli and garlic floats up the spiral staircase and I automatically lick my lips in anticipation. Lianna stayed at The Hangout and isn't coming back until tomorrow, so it's just the six of us tonight. To be honest, I am secretly glad as it gives us free rein to talk about Vernon without holding back.

Taking my seat at the marble dining table, I greet the others with a kiss on the cheek before accepting a glass of fizz from Eve. Always the hostess with the mostess. Eve could even make Nigella look unaccommodating. Sipping the ice-cold bubbles, I raise a hand in acknowledgement to James. I am about to ask him how on earth he manages to cook a three-course meal for six people single-handedly when I spot his sous chef buzzing around the kitchen. I watch the two of them laughing merrily and can't help but smile. We could all do with taking a bit of the happy go luckily Bajan spirit home with us.

Turning my attention to Marc, I ask him how his day of babysitting went.

'We actually had a lot of fun.' Pushing his glasses up the bridge of his nose, he reaches for his drink. 'Madison chased the pelicans all afternoon and MJ ate his weight in ice cream.'

Gina flashes him a disapproving look and shakes her head. 'If he vomits later, *you're* cleaning it up.'

'And if *you* vomit later, *you're* cleaning it up.' Marc takes the glass of fizz out of Gina's hand and places it on the table out of her reach.

I let out a little laugh and disguise it with a cough when Gina shoots me a glare.

'So...' Owen smiles and leans back in his seat. 'I believe that Vernon got the royal seal of approval?'

'He did.' I confirm happily. 'I hate to admit it, but Eve was right.'

'I told you!' Eve trills, handing out bowls of spicy nuts. 'I think they are perfect for each other.' Her eyes mist over and I bite my lip to stop myself from pointing out that long-distance relationships almost never work out.

Don't get me wrong, I like Vernon. I like him a lot. I'd even go as far as to say that he would be ideal for Li, *if* he lived in the same country. Taking a handful of nuts, I nibble in silence as Owen rambles about what a good guy Vernon is. Apparently, he is quite a popular man on the island. It seems that everybody worth knowing knows Vernon Clarke.

'I loved him.' Gina gushes through a mouthful of nuts. 'And Stephanie, she was great, too.'

'Stephanie?' Eve's brow creases in confusion as she helps James bring over our starters.

'His new bar manager.' I clarify, taking a steaming plate of scallops and mouthing *thank you* to James.

'He finally found someone?' Owen asks. 'That's great. The last time I spoke to him he was really struggling to hire someone.'

'Apparently, he had to poach Stephanie from a rival restaurant.' I raise my eyebrows tellingly and pick up my fork.

'That's a little controversial, isn't it?' Marc adjusts the volume of the baby monitor and thanks James for his food.

'It's just business.' Gina hiccups and reaches for the water jug. 'You can't take it personally.'

'Do you know which restaurant she worked at?' Owen asks as he tucks into his starter.

'I think he said it was called... *Driftwood*.' I say uncertainly. 'I can't be sure though.'

'Driftwood...' He repeats. 'You ever heard of Driftwood, James?'

'Down on the beach?' James asks, drying his hands on a tea towel. 'Yeah, I know it. They must be paying her some serious money to leave that place. It's one of the busiest bars on the island.'

'Really?' Eve asks between mouthfuls. 'Why have I never heard of it?'

'It's very exclusive.' James winks. 'Members only.'

Obviously stunned into silence at the discovery of an exclusive bar that she is not a member of, Eve frowns and turns her attention to her food. I swallow a smile and chew my scallop carefully. I didn't think there was an exclusive establishment in the world which Eve didn't have a VIP card for. Resisting the urge to lick my plate clean, I put down my cutlery and flash James the thumbs-up sign. He really is a fabulous cook. I don't know what's more impressive, having a live-in chef or the villa itself.

'What's everyone got planned for tomorrow?' Owen asks, wiping his mouth with a napkin.

'I thought we could go shopping!' Eve squeals, clapping her hands together and smiling happily.

Holding her hands up in protest, Gina shakes her head. 'If it doesn't involve a sun lounger, rum, or the beach then I'm not doing it.'

'Oh, come on!' Eve pleads, reaching for her handbag and pulling out a wad of leaflets. 'Look! There's a fantastic shopping centre right here on the west coast!'

'Not doing it.' Gina sticks to her guns and folds her arms defensively. 'Do you have any idea how many shops you drag me around back home?'

Eve purses her lips for a moment before putting away her leaflets in defeat.

'I'll go with you.' I offer her a friendly smile and take a sip of my bubbles.

'There you go.' Owen reaches over and strokes his wife's arm.

Holding up my hands, I flash Eve a wink and lean back in my seat. 'There's just one condition. I'll go with you... *if* Oliver and Owen watch the children...'

A look of dismay washes over their faces as they stare at me in horror.

'But... but we had planned on a snorkelling trip tomorrow.' Oliver shoots me a *please let me* go look, but I shake my head in response.

'You boys have been having *all* the fun.' Eve chips in. 'This is the most that I have seen of the pair of you since we arrived.'

Looking at each other guilty, they sit in silence for a moment before Owen speaks up. 'Fair enough. You girls go shopping.'

'Yes!' I give Eve a high five and mouth *thank you* at my husband.

Watching his handsome face fall, I find myself feeling a little bad. 'Don't look at me like that. You have had your fun and now I can have mine...'

* * *

Ouch! This is *not* my idea of fun. Biting my lip to stop myself from shouting out in pain, I curse myself for letting Eve talk me into this. A lovely morning of retail therapy followed by a cooling Frappuccino in the sunshine quickly turned into my worst nightmare. Holding up a hand to stop Eve from taking photographs, I mentally curse her into oblivion.

'Almost done.' The plump lady murmurs, taking the final pieces of my hair and tugging on them tightly.

When you have a badly burnt scalp, cornrows are probably not the wisest hairstyle choice. Hearing Eve giggle, I shoot her daggers and exhale loudly.

'Finished.' The jolly hairdresser announces proudly. Holding up a mirror, she flashes me a huge smile. 'Looks good, yeah?'

My mouth drops open as I look at my reflection. Not knowing what to say, I gasp loudly and nod in response. Every scrap of hair on my head has been tightly bound into dozens of little braids. I look bald. I look completely bald. Don't ask me how, because all my hair is still there, but you can actually see my scalp. My very burnt, very sore scalp.

Handing the hairdresser a wad of notes, I scramble to my feet and shove Eve into the seat. 'Your turn.'

'What?' Eve laughs and attempts to stand up, but I sit on top of her and shake my head.

'As a thank you for inviting us out here, I would like to pay for this for you.' I smile sweetly and pass over more cash.

'There's really no need.' Eve protests. 'Besides, my hair probably isn't long enough.' She looks up at the hairdresser hopefully.

Unfortunately for Eve, she shakes her head starts grabbing sections of Eve's platinum blonde bob. 'We can get a few in here.'

Hiding behind my phone to disguise my laughter, I jab on the camera icon and snap away. A look of sheer terror washes over her face as her hair is pulled back tightly into neat braids. Not so funny now, is it? Hearing the fluorescent pink beads bang together as my head bobs around as I giggle, I drop my phone into my handbag and point to the tray of beads.

'I think the green ones would look *great* with Eve's skin tone.' I smile devilishly and suppress a giggle.

'Actually, green isn't really my colour...' She looks into the tray and frowns as she realises that green is probably the best of a bad bunch. 'But I guess I could give it a go.'

The hairdresser nods in agreement and proceeds to thread a selection of lime coloured gems into Eve's hair. Unlike my full of head of braids, Eve has escaped with just ten, five on each side but she looks equally as ridiculous. Thanking the stylist, we gather our shopping bags and make our way outside. Once I am sure that we are safely out of earshot, I turn to Eve and hit her on the arm.

'Happy now? Look at the state of us!' I attempt to keep my face serious, but Eve looks so comical that it is almost impossible.

A giggle starts to grow in the pit of my stomach and I try desperately to control it. Pursing her lips, she reaches up and touches her braids gently. Her eyes turning to saucers as her hand lands on bare scalp.

'Well?' I persist, folding my arms.

Opening her mouth to speak, she resorts to a shrug of the shoulders before bursting into hysterics. Unable to hold in my own laughter for any longer, I lean against the shop front as my stomach throbs with glee. People are starting to stare, but I just can't control myself. Why the hell did I let her talk me into this?

'Come on.' Wiping away the laughter tears, I shake my head so that my beads jangle together. 'Let's go and get a drink...'

Chapter 8

'Well?' Eve and I stand in the kitchen and point to our new hairstyles proudly. 'What do you think?'

I look around the room at the blank faces staring back at me, not surprisingly it's Gina that laughs first.

'What the *hell* happened to you two?' She jumps to her feet and runs across the kitchen. 'I can actually *see* your scalp!'

Joining in with her laughter, I throw my arms around Eve's neck and jangle her beads. The three glasses of rum punch we had earlier have made the cornrows situation seem a whole lot funnier than it did a few hours ago. In fact, I am actually starting to like my new look; even if the beads *do* hurt my ears when they bang together.

Sliding out of Marc's arms, Madison throws her book on the floor and scuttles over. 'You look silly!' She points a finger at the pair of us and erupts into a fit of giggles.

'I think Madison speaks on behalf of all of us.' Owen mumbles, taking a sip of his beer.

Copying his sister, MJ laughs and begs to be picked up, only to tug on Eve's plaits like a naughty little monkey. Prising him away and sitting him on her hip, Gina grabs Madison with her free hand.

'Who wants to have a final dip in the sea before the sun goes down?'

'*Me!*' They squeal in unison as they fight like crazy to get down.

Letting them loose, Gina grabs some sun cream from the kitchen island and runs out onto the balcony.

'Those things aren't permanent, are they?' Oliver pipes up from his place on the couch. 'You look like a pair of Avatars.'

'I seriously hope not.' I reach up and attempt to free my hair from the ridiculously tight braids.

A good few minutes and a lot of painful pulls later, my tangled hair springs to life. I don't even need to look in a mirror to realise that I am now rocking an extreme version of the 90's crimped look.

Wincing as my scalp stings like crazy, I kick off my sandals and make my way over to the couch. The cold tiles feel like heaven on my sore soles. An entire day of walking around the shopping centre has taken its toll on my poor tootsies and all I want to do now is snuggle up with my boys. Planting a kiss on Oliver's cheeks, I pluck Noah out of his arms and curl up next to him.

'How has your day been?' I ask, throwing Noah up into the air and laughing as he squeals.

Oliver frowns and attempts to remove the rest of my braids. 'Can you take those things out of your hair, please? I really can't take you seriously while you look like that.'

'You don't like them?' I tease. 'I was thinking we could get yours done, too...'

He eyes up my hair dubiously and lets out a laugh. 'I don't think so.'

Handing over Noah, I set to work at removing the remaining braids from my hair.

'You can't take them all out!' Eve exclaims in dismay. 'We have to keep them until the end of the holiday!'

'You have to be kidding me!' I shake my head in response and tug out the last one. 'Are you seriously keeping yours?'

'I might do...' She shakes her head and jangles her beads together.

'I think that's the rum talking.' I mumble to Oliver, hoping that she feels different once she has sobered up. 'I should get in the shower before Lianna arrives with Vernon.'

'Then you better shower lightning quick.' Owen chuckles. 'They're at the gates right now.'

Feeling a little mortified at the thought of Vernon seeing me with hair like a deranged scarecrow, I frantically run my fingers through my tangled mane in a desperate bid to make myself look respectable.

'What's the plan for dinner?' I ask, suddenly realising that James isn't around.

'I thought we could have a barbecue down on the beach.' Eve takes a bottle of water from the fridge and slides onto a stool.

'Great idea!' I tickle Noah's stomach and breathe a secret sigh of relief.

As delicious as James' food is, I am a little relieved to have a break from rich cuisine for the evening. A flame-grilled burger and an ice-cold beer sounds pretty perfect if you ask me. Hearing Lianna's familiar laugh flood into the room, I look up to see my best friend falling through the doorway in a bubble of giggles. Flashing her a smile, I offer them a wave as Vernon follows in behind her.

Watching Eve and Owen embrace the pair of them warmly, I can't help but think what a lovely couple they make. I don't just mean physically either, they actually seem to make each other incredibly happy.

Standing up to greet them, I plant a kiss on Lianna's cheek and pass her Noah, who is eagerly trying to climb over to his favourite auntie. Blowing a raspberry on his stomach, Li turns him upside down and laughs as he shrieks like an excited monkey.

'Come over here, there are some people that I want you to meet.' Her eyes twinkle as she takes Vernon's hand and leads him over to where Oliver and Marc are sitting.

Immediately standing to attention, Oliver and Marc jump to their feet and hold out their hands. In true Marc fashion, he smiles thinly and nods as he shakes Vernon's hand.

'Hey.' Oliver smiles widely and claps him on the back.

'A fellow American?' Vernon asks, a relieved smile playing on the corner of his lips. 'No way!'

Flashing Oliver a wink, I smile to myself as I watch them talk. It must be nice for Oliver to hear another American accent. He doesn't really talk about it, but I know that he misses Texas and his family across the pond. Leaving the boys to get acquainted, I link my arm through Lianna's and lead her outside into the sunshine. From our position on the veranda, we can see Gina with Madison and MJ playing in the water. Hearing his friends having fun, Noah instantly struggles to get down and join them.

'Do you want to take him down?' Lianna mumbles, stretching out her legs.

Noah lets out an almighty scream and thrashes around like a fish out of water. 'I don't think I've got much choice. You coming?'

Li looks over her shoulder and flashes Vernon a smile. 'I should probably stay with Vern and make sure the boys don't pick on him.'

'Don't be ridiculous!' I scoff, pushing her towards the sand. 'He's a big boy. I am sure he can look after himself.'

Popping our heads back into the villa, she nods in agreement as she realises that the boys are already bonding over beer and baseball. Poor Marc. He's trying *so* hard to look interested, but I know that he would rather be down at the beach talking nails and cocktails given half the chance. Flashing him a wink, I kick off my sandals and grab Noah's hat from the deck chair.

'So, how has your day been?' I ask, waving at Madison as we make our way down the beach.

Lianna exhales loudly and twists her hair up into a messy top knot. 'We had a bit of a disaster in the kitchen...'

'Disaster?' I scrunch up my nose and frown. 'What kind of disaster?'

Bending down to pick up a shell, she turns it over in her hands before slipping it into her back pocket. 'Someone mixed up an order and we ended up with a ton of fish that we didn't ask for.'

'Uh oh. How did that happen?' Noah pulls off his sunglasses and chews on the end happily.

'I have *no* idea...'

Her voice trails off as we come to stop at the water's edge.

'No idea about what?' Gina asks as she blows up MJ's tiny armbands.

Stripping off my dress, I hand Noah to Li and wade into the warm sea. Madison demands to be picked up, so I sit her on my shoulders as Li fills Gina in on her kitchen catastrophe. Apparently, if it wasn't for Stephanie, The Hangout would have been in almighty trouble today. It looks like poaching Stephanie was worth it after all.

Holding Madison's legs up so that she can pretend to swim, I look along the shoreline at the volleyball contest further up the beach. Dozens of people dive into the sand, their laughter drifting along the beach as the crowd cheers them on. As nice as it is to be nestled away in a secluded corner of the beach, it would be fun to experience a livelier atmosphere for a change. Making a mental note to arrange this with the others, I talk Madison into shell hunting with her brother so that the grown-ups can talk.

'What's going on with your hair by the way?' Li asks, tossing her own locks over one shoulder. 'Why have you got the whole Diana Ross thing going on?'

Shooting her daggers, I pull a bobble from my wrist and force my impromptu afro into something that resembles a bun. I wondered how long it would be before someone mentioned the hair. Not wanting to be the focus of their jokes, I change the subject to Vernon.

'How do you think the boys are getting on?' I whisper, grabbing a handful of sand and rubbing it into my thighs.

'Great by the looks of things.' Gina bobs her head in the direction of the villa as we all spin around to have a look.

Clutching bottles of beer, the four of them study the barbecue as though it is made of gold. What is it with men and fire? I don't think I have ever seen Oliver look so excited. Marc, on the other hand, is nodding along attentively, desperately trying to be one of the boys.

'Do you think they like him?' Li asks, biting her lip anxiously and handing over Noah.

Obviously tiring of tugging on Lianna's hair, he reaches up and takes a handful of mine and pulls hard. *Ouch!* When the hell is he going to grow out of that?

'How can you *not* like him?' Gina scoffs, throwing back her head and cackling like a hyena.

'I hate to admit it, but he is pretty perfect.' I lock eyes with Lianna and nod in agreement. 'So, how's this going to pan out between the two of you?'

'What do you mean?' She picks a pink shell out of the sand and hands it to Madison.

'The whole *long-distance* thing.' As soon as the words escape my mouth I wonder if I have done the right thing by bringing it up, but I can tell from the look on Gina's face that she has been thinking the same thing.

She shrugs her shoulders nonchalantly and slides into the water. 'I haven't really thought about it.'

Gina and I exchange glances and I can't resist probing the subject further. 'You must have *spoken* about it though.'

Li screws up her nose and floats around casually. 'Not really.'

Flashing her a thin smile, I tell myself to shut up. Her cool as a cucumber attitude towards this relationship is really getting on my nerves, but I don't want to ruin things by creating an awkward atmosphere between us. Hearing footsteps behind me, I look over my shoulder to see Vernon striding over the sand. Thanking my lucky stars that I shut up when I did, I smile as Vernon takes a seat next to Lianna.

'How are you guys doing?' He takes a sip from his beer bottle and wedges it into the sand.

Eyeing him up carefully, Madison holds out her tiny hand. 'I'm Madison Milan Stroker.'

Trying not to laugh, I watch as Vernon takes her hand and shakes it gently. 'It's a pleasure to meet you, Madison *Milan* Stroker.'

'Do you want to collect shells with me?' She holds out her pink bucket to show him her collection.

'Sure.' His eyes widen as Madison places her bucket between them and instructs him on what to do. 'And who is this little guy?' He ruffles MJ's long curls and tosses a shell into the bucket.

'This is Marc Junior.' Gina smiles and pushes MJ forward. 'Say hello, MJ.'

'MJ.' Vernon repeats and shoots him a wink. 'Cool name.'

Cautiously making his way over, MJ sits down next to his sister and smiles warily. It seems that MJ hasn't inherited Gina's bolshie, fearless attitude like Madison. Sitting Noah on the sand between my legs, I grab a bottle of water from Gina's beach bag and take a sip, grimacing when I realise it's warmer than the sea.

'How were the boys?' Lianna asks, slipping an arm around Vernon's waist. 'Did they play nice?'

He laughs and nods in response. 'Very nice. I actually invited them to the bar tomorrow for the fish fry.' He digs a shell out of the water and adds it to MJ's pile. 'That invitation is extended to all of you, in case that wasn't clear.'

'And me?' Madison asks, kicking her legs in excitement.

MJ copies his sister and throws his arms in the air.

'Yeah, you guys, too.' Vernon laughs and whips off his t-shirt to reveal an incredible six-pack. 'I'm going for a dip. Who's with me?'

Madison waves her hands around and runs in after him as MJ throws an almighty tantrum at not being able to join them without his armbands on. Throwing Madison onto his shoulders, Vernon wades into the water and playfully splashes her with water. He's certainly fantastic with kids, that's for sure. My mother once told me that if you ever want to know if a person has a good heart, watch how they are with children. If that's the case, then Vernon's a definite keeper.

The distinctive smell of charcoal floats down from the villa and I flare my nostrils greedily.

'Who wants a burger?' Owen yells, waving his spatula around in the air.

Not missing a beat, MJ dives out of Gina's arms and runs across the sand as fast as his little legs will carry him. My stomach starts to grumble and I realise that I haven't eaten a thing since breakfast.

'Are you coming up for some food?' Gina asks, as though reading my mind.

Nodding in response, I push myself to my feet and peel Noah away from the sandcastle. I am about to ask if Lianna is joining us when she strips off her top and dives into the water. Unless she is planning on spearing some fish, she won't be eating in there. Deciding to leave the love birds alone for a while, I leave Gina to retrieve Madison and make my way back to the villa.

Obviously having had second thoughts on the cornrows, Eve has removed the braids and set her now crazy curls free. I think we can safely say that we won't be doing *that* again. Placing Noah into a highchair, I grab a plate and fill it with a selection of bread, salad and dips. Biting on a celery stick, I tear up some bread and give it to Noah before taking a seat on Oliver's lap.

The sun has started to dip in the sky, casting a beautiful shadow over the veranda. Watching Owen and Marc flip burgers as the children wait patiently with their plastic plates, I dip a breadstick into a mound of garlic dip and chew happily. Seeing him chase Li around in the water a wave of relief washes over me. As much as it kills me to say it, I was wrong about Vernon. Normally I hate being proved wrong, but for the first time in my life, being wrong feels so very right...

Chapter 9

Walking across the hot sand, I smooth down my jumpsuit and follow behind Owen and Eve as they lead the way to The Hangout. The moon is high in the sky, throwing a strip of light across the beach. After a long day of sunbathing and stuffing my face with James' fabulous flying fish, I could very easily have spent the evening snoozing on a sun lounger. Not wanting to let down Li, I forced myself to change into something respectable and applied a slick of ruby red to my lips. Fortunately, it appears that my laziness isn't contagious. Oliver seems to have formed quite the bromance with Vernon and has been itching to get to The Hangout all afternoon.

Turning the corner, I must admit that The Hangout looks a little different to how I remember it. The hammocks that line the entrance are filled with beautiful people who are happily kicking back with a cocktail or three. Spotting a couple of security guards at the door, I pick up Noah and entwine my fingers with Oliver's. Hoping they don't tell us that we aren't on the guest list, I raise my hand and smile as I spot Lianna weaving her way through the crowd. Unclicking the red rope, she smiles brightly and beckons us inside. Wow! This place sure looks a lot different than I remember it. Twinkling fairy lights light up the black sky, indicating to the world that The Hangout is the *only* place to be right now.

Holding out my arms for a hug, I plant a kiss on her cheek as she leads us through to a booth. Noticing that she has even put out highchairs for Noah and Melrose, I mouth *thank you* at her and slide into my seat.

'Very nice.' Gina nods in approval and plucks a menu from the table. 'Where's Vernon?'

'Erm...' Li scratches her nose and looks around the busy bar. 'He's around here... somewhere! You guys get comfortable and I'll go fetch you some drinks.'

Realising that she knows half of the people in here, Eve excuses herself to mingle with the other customers. Watching her float from table to table like a social butterfly, I take the opportunity to scan the room. The breeze from the ocean causes the palm trees to rustle gently as reggae music fills the open space. I glance at a stunning young couple swaying to the music in an adjacent booth and can't help but smile. Completely lost in each other's arms, they seem totally oblivious to the fact that they are in a busy bar surrounded by other customers. Tearing my eyes away, I stroke Noah's hair and turn my attention to Marc. With Oliver and Owen lost in boy talk and Gina chatting away to Stephanie, he looks a little lost.

'Are you alright?' I ask, prodding him in the ribs.

He pushes his glasses up the bridge of his nose and smiles. 'I'm in Barbados, of course I'm alright.'

Not convinced, I squint my eyes at him suspiciously. 'What do you think of Vernon?'

'I think he's great.' Marc fires back, not missing a beat. 'Really great. To be honest, I was expecting another idiot. Let's face it, Li seems to attract nothing but losers.'

I nod in response and giggle to myself, silently recalling the many, *many* men that Lianna has deemed to be *The One*. From the almost perfect Pablo to the frankly disastrous Dan, it seems that it could be a case of third time lucky for our best friend.

The music turns up a notch as a flurry of new people floats into the bar. There is such a strange mix of people in here. From locals with their families, to glamorous tourists and the odd 'could be' celebrity. It seems that The Hangout attracts a wide range of clientele.

'Hey, guys!' Vernon's now familiar voice pierces my thought bubble, bringing me back to earth with a thud.

Smiling as Oliver and Owen jump up to greet him, I wait until they have put him down before offering my cheek for a kiss.

'How's it going?' Vernon flashes us his usual big smile, but I can tell that he seems a little preoccupied.

'We're good.' Gina answers on behalf of us and pulls Madison onto her knee. 'How are you?'

'I'm alright.' He scratches his nose and reaches down to give Noah a high five. 'We're gonna start the fish fry soon, you guys hungry?'

Madison and MJ squeal with delight at the prospect of food and I can't help but laugh.

'Oliver, could I borrow you real quick?' He motions outside as Oliver nods and slides out of the booth.

Exchanging confused glances with Gina, I turn my attention to Owen. 'What's going on there?'

'Don't ask me!' Owen chuckles, watching the two of them walk away. 'I'm as clueless as the rest of you.'

I'm about to give him the third degree when Li reappears with a tray of drinks. Accepting a tall glass of rum punch, I take a sip and slide over to make room for her to join us.

'You've certainly found your way around the place.' I tease, twirling my straw around my glass.

'Someone's getting their feet well and truly under the table.' Gina cackles loudly and prods her in the ribs.

Lianna's cheeks flush pink and she chooses to ignore us. 'Where's Oliver?' She asks, looking around the table and realising that he's missing.

'Erm, he went somewhere with Vernon.' I point outside and shrug my shoulders.

'Oh...' She frowns and glances around the bar. 'Do you know where to?'

Shaking my head in response, I chew on the end of my straw and wonder when the fish fry will open. I am daydreaming of yummy barbecued treats when I spot Oliver weaving his way through the sea of people. I can tell by the worried look on his face that something is wrong. Flashing him a quizzical look, I am about to ask him where he has been when he taps Lianna on the shoulder.

'Li, Vern would like to talk to you.' Oliver wipes a bead of sweat from his brow and takes a big gulp of his drink.

'OK...' She mumbles, understandably confused.

'He's outside.' Avoiding all eye contact, he pulls Noah from his highchair and hands him a bottle of water.

The entire table falls silent as we watch Lianna walk away. For a moment none of us speaks, we just sit in an awkward silence. My stomach flips as I chew the inside of my cheek anxiously. This does not sound good. Finally, Gina speaks up.

'What the hell is going on here?' She demands, banging her hand down on the table.

Looking over his shoulder to ensure that Li is out of earshot, he lets out a huge sigh and runs a hand through his hair. 'I'm sure you'll find out soon enough.'

'Oliver!' Starting to feel worried, I hit him on the arm. 'Tell me!'

Obviously not wanting to spill the beans, he opens and closes his mouth repeatedly. Not being able to stay in my seat, I put down my drink and make my way through the crowd, quickly followed by Gina. Squinting my eyes, I slip outside and weave through the hammocks. The fact that it's so dark makes it near impossible to see more than a few feet in front of you. Following the moonlight along the sand, I finally spot the two of them at the water's edge.

'There they are!' I whisper to Gina, kicking off my sandals and creeping across the sand.

Coming to a stop behind a palm tree, I hold a finger to my lips. The waves crash against the sand, meaning that I can't hear a word that they're saying. *Please don't be breaking up with her.* Peeking around the trunk, I let out a gasp as I realise that Vernon is down on one knee. *Is he?* My jaw drops in shock as I take in the scene in front of me.

'What's going on?' Gina demands, shoving me out of the way so that she can see.

'Yes!' Lianna screams loudly, catching the attention of the hammock loungers. 'Yes! Yes! Yes! Of course, I will marry you!'

A round of applause echoes around the beach as the crowd erupts into whoops and cheers. Steadying myself on Gina's shoulder, my heart pounds erratically in my chest. Li's squeals echo around the bay as people begin to run over and congratulate them. Tearing her arm from mine, Gina joins in and dashes over the sand. Watching the hordes of people surrounding the happy couple, I regain the use of my legs and slowly amble over to join them.

Catching my eye, Lianna squeezes her way through the masses and throws her arms around my neck.

'I'm engaged!' She yells, so loudly that I'm surprised she doesn't burst my eardrum. 'I'm engaged! I'm engaged! I'm engaged!'

'I can see that...' I laugh nervously, snatching her hands for a glimpse of the ring.

Pulling her to one side, I hold her ring finger up to the moonlight and let out a gasp.

'Oh, Lianna!' Running my fingers over the enormous sapphire ring, my stomach churns uncontrollably. The incredible blue gemstone is held in a classic gold setting and surrounded by delicate diamond clusters. 'It's stunning. It really is beautiful.'

Tearing himself away from the well-wishers, Vernon runs up behind Li and throws her into the air as though she is as light as a kitten. As people drift out of the bar to see what all the cheering is about, I spot Oliver at the entrance with Noah on his hip. Making my way over to him, I scoop up Madison as she rushes along the sand.

'Did you know about this?' I ask, as Madison climbs onto my back.

'Only five minutes before you did!' He laughs and moves to the side to make room for Owen and Eve.

'What is going on out here?' Eve giggles, hitching up her dress and creeping across the decking.

'Lianna and Vernon are engaged!' Gina screeches, pointing behind her as the two of them walk hand in hand along the shore.

'Awwh!' Eve exclaims, clapping her hands together and running over to them. 'This is *amazing!*'

Feeling a little lost for words, I shoot Oliver a concerned glance and bite my lip. Engaged. Engaged to be married. Engaged to be married to someone she has spent approximately ten days with. Telling myself not to be pessimistic, I stretch my lips into a thin smile. Oliver throws an arm around my waist as Owen heads off after Eve. Watching my friends rejoice happily, I make a mental promise to myself to keep my opinions on the subject hidden.

Who am I to judge whether or not this is the right thing for Li? She's a big girl and can make her own decisions. Reminding myself that I fell too hard, too fast for Oliver, I twirl my wedding band around my finger and exhale slowly. My mother once told me that you don't find love, love finds you. There's no logic to it and once it has a hold of you, there's no going back. I guess love doesn't have to be perfect, it just has to be true...

Chapter 10

Devouring my second spicy fish burger, I lick a dollop of chilli sauce from my finger and kick off my sandals under the table. It has been a few hours since Vernon decided to pop the question and it has been the subject on everybody's lips ever since. Between regular customers stopping by our booth to pass on their congratulations and Gina firing a million questions at the happy couple, no one else has managed to get a word in.

'What made you go for a sapphire ring?'

'When did you realise that you were going to propose?'

'Will you get married here in Barbados?'

That last one catches my attention and I look up from my drink.

'Well...' Vernon starts, smiling down on his new fiancée. 'We haven't had the chance to speak about it, but I thought we could do it right here.'

'Here?' Lianna's eyes light up as she looks around The Hangout.

Turning her head gently, Vernon points outside to the beach. 'There.'

'Awwh!' Eve sighs, holding a tissue to her eyes. 'That would be so romantic.'

'When?' Gina asks, watching the children play hide and seek around the bar.

'That part is down to you.' Vern whispers to Li.

Looking down at her shiny new ring, Lianna runs her fingers over the gold band and smiles. 'How about right now?'

The entire table bursts into laughter as Vernon shakes his head. 'I think the Ministry of Home Affairs might need a little more time than that.'

'Tomorrow?' She fires back. 'The next day?'

'What's the rush?' I ask, causing the rest of the group to flash me daggers. 'What?' I retort. 'It takes months if not years to plan a wedding!'

'Not necessarily...' Vernon interrupts. 'We often have weddings here and depending on what it is you want; they can be arranged in a matter of days.'

'I could help!' Eve yells, raising her hand like a child in the classroom.

'And me!' Digging Gina in the ribs, I hold up my hands in protest.

'Li, can I talk to you for a moment... privately?' Handing over Noah to Oliver, I smile apologetically at Owen as I squeeze my big bum past him.

Motioning for Lianna to follow me, I slip outside and climb into a vacant hammock. Thankfully, the crowds have dispersed and all that remains are a final few couples enjoying the moonlight. Watching Lianna practically float across the sand, I hate myself for what I am about to say. Waiting until she is settled into the opposite hammock, I take a deep breath before I speak.

'Lianna, you *can't* get married right now. You know that, don't you?' Twisting my hair up into a messy bun, I study her face as she smiles back at me. 'Don't get me wrong, I like Vernon. We all like him, but *marriage?* You have spent less than two weeks together. Don't you think you should get to know each other a little better first?'

'I *am* going to marry him, Clara.' She leans back in her hammock and stretches out her legs, obviously not taking a word that I am saying seriously.

'OK...' I mumble, realising that I am going to have to try a different path here. 'I just don't understand why you have to marry him right away, that's all. Let's face it, we have been here before, remember?'

'I do remember.' She laughs heartily and rocks her hammock from side to side. 'How could I forget?'

'Then *why* are you rushing into this?' I exclaim, throwing my hands into the air. 'Haven't you learnt *anything* from all of your other disasters?' As soon as the words escape my lips, I wish I could take them back. 'I'm sorry. I don't want to ruin this for you. I'm just looking out for you. You're my best friend and I would be doing you a major disservice if I were to let this happen and not voice my concerns.'

Hopping out of her hammock, Li shoves me over and climbs in next to me. Slightly concerned that she is going to make us capsize, I hold onto the rope for dear life. Reaching into her pocket, she pulls out a shiny grey pebble and places it into my hand. *What the hell is this?* I think to myself, turning it over in my hands.

'It's a proposal pebble.' Li declares, as though reading my mind. 'Isn't it beautiful?'

'Beautiful?' I repeat, holding up the stone for a better look. 'Lianna, it's a stone.'

Rolling her eyes, she snatches the stone out of my hands and polishes it on her t-shirt. 'You know how much I love penguins, right?'

'Right...' I mumble, worrying that she has completely lost her mind.

'Well, penguins propose to each other with pebbles.' She giggles like a baby and smiles brightly.

'How much of that punch have you had?' I lean over the hammock and realise that her glass is still full.

'When a penguin falls in love with another penguin, he searches the entire beach to find the most perfect pebble. It has to be just right, like the perfect engagement ring.' Her eyes gloss over as she tosses her hair over her shoulder. 'It might take him days, it might take him weeks, but when he finally finds it, he waddles over to his beloved and places it right in front of her. Just like a proposal.'

Not wanting to admit that this is very possibly the cutest thing I have ever heard, I look down at my feet as my face involuntarily stretches into a smile.

'So, what are you saying? That Vernon proposed to you with a pebble?'

'That's exactly what I'm saying.' Popping the pebble back into her pocket, she twists her engagement ring around her finger and smiles. 'And the fact that he backed it up with a three-carat sapphire ring just makes him even more perfect.'

Letting out an exasperated sigh, I run my fingers through my hair and shake my head. 'It sounds like you have already made your mind up on this.'

'I have.' She nods in agreement and holds out her little finger. 'The only question left is... are you *in* or are you *out?*'

* * *

'Did you manage to change the flights?' Gina asks, as Marc comes into the living room with a handful of papers.

'Uh-huh.' He mumbles, sifting through the pile and placing it on the coffee table. 'We now have another six days.'

'Yay!' Madison cries, jumping up and down. 'Another six days!'

'What date are we looking at again?' Eve flips open a notepad starts scribbling away. 'The thirteenth?'

'Fourteenth.' Lianna corrects from her position on the floor.

As it is almost forty degrees outside, we have decided to take a break from the sunshine to cool down in the villa. With the adults busy planning Lianna's impromptu wedding, James took it upon himself to rustle up a quick lunch. Now that we are suitably fed and watered, we can fully concentrate on the task at hand, which isn't as easy as it sounds with four hyper children running around the place. Rubbing my throbbing temples, I push myself to my feet and try to gather my thoughts. High on sugar, Madison fires through the living room and knocks the pile of paperwork onto the floor. Letting out an annoyed sigh, I bend down and attempt to put the many sheets of paper back in order.

'Marc, could you take the children out for the afternoon? We aren't going to get far with four kids under our feet.' I flash him a hopeful smile and pray that he doesn't refuse.

'All of them?' He groans, collapsing into an armchair as Melrose crashes into his legs in her baby walker.

'I'll come with you.' Oliver sighs. 'To be honest, I've had enough of the wedding talk.' Scooping up Noah, he slips on his flip-flops and grabs his baseball cap from the floor.

'Me, too.' Owen yawns, rolling off the couch. 'Why don't we leave you girls to do your thing and get the kids out of your hair?'

Not missing a beat, Eve and Gina immediately gather up the children and usher them towards the door. Obviously glad to be escaping the wedding club, Marc packs a bag with child-friendly essentials as Owen searches for his car keys. Kissing Oliver and Noah goodbye, I walk across the warm tiles and watch them climb into Owen's car. Waving them off, I watch the car do a three-point turn on the driveway before pulling out into the road. The palm trees outside are completely still, meaning that there isn't even a whiff of a breeze. Quickly closing the door, I retreat into the air-conditioned room and breathe a sigh of relief.

Grabbing a bottle of water from the fridge, I prop myself up at the breakfast bar and peek at Eve's notepad. Unlike Li's previous wedding plans, this time she is going for casual and taking a more laid-back approach to the whole affair. According to her very short list of demands, she wants to get married at sunset, in anything that's white, with Melrose, Madison, Gina, Eve and myself as bridesmaids. Apart from those things, she really doesn't seem to care about the rest.

'And you're sure that you don't want to call your parents?' Eve asks, tapping her pen on the marble countertop. 'We could get them on the next flight out here?'

Shaking her head in response, Li runs her hands through her hair and lets it fall around her shoulders. 'My mum is in New York with her friends and my dad would never be able to take time off work at such short notice. They would only give me a hard time about it anyway.'

A wave of worry flashes over Eve's face before she shakes it off in favour of a smile. As worried as I am that Lianna is rushing into this marriage, I'm not concerned in the least about her not having her parents here. For those of you who don't know, Vanessa Edwards or Vanessa Parker as she is known since the divorce, is not your typical cookie-cutter mother and I think it's safe to say that she wouldn't be too bothered about missing Li's impromptu nuptials. The same goes for her father, don't get me wrong he's lovely, but he would rather chop off his own legs than miss a business meeting. Confident that she won't regret her decision, I indicate to Eve to move on to the next thing on her list.

'What about catering? She asks, scribbling something in her notepad. 'I could hire James for you as a wedding gift?'

'Actually, I think Vernon has already asked Patricia.' Li smiles apologetically at James and sticks out her bottom lip. 'You're more than welcome to come along to the wedding though, James. We would love to have you there.'

'Really?' James laughs, obviously touched at the invitation.

'Really!' Joining in with the laughter, she shields her eyes from the sun and rolls onto her stomach. 'The more the merrier.'

James' cheeks flush pink and he nods his head gratefully. He really is the cutest.

'That brings me onto the guest list.' Eve sighs and chews her pen. 'Who do you want to be there?'

'You guys.' Lianna fires back, as though the answer couldn't be more obvious.

'And what about Vernon's side?'

'Oh, don't worry about Vernon's side. He is going to deal with all that.'

Letting out an exasperated sigh, Eve puts down her pen and shakes her head. 'Lianna, do you have any idea how difficult it is to plan a wedding when you don't know how many people are attending?'

Pushing herself to her feet, Li squeezes between us and plucks the notepad out of Eve's hands. After studying the paper for a moment, she takes a pen and crosses everything off the list, before circling just one bullet point. Handing Eve back the notepad she points to the last thing on the list.

'Let me get this straight. You are getting married in six days, and the only thing you need us to do is get you a dress?' Eve's brow furrows as she drops the notepad onto the countertop.

'It doesn't have to be a dress.' Lianna muses, twirling her ring around her finger. 'As long as it's white, I'm really not that bothered...'

* * *

A couple of hours and more than a few rum punches later, we seem to have all the arrangements in place. Unfortunately, Li had to dash off to The Hangout a few moments ago after a frantic phone call from Vernon. Apparently, there has been some sort of mix-up with the VIP guest list and one of their regular celebrity clients has kicked up a storm. Oh, the joys of dealing with the A-List. Gina and I did try to make a joke of it, but it seems that upsetting the superstar clientele is a big no-no.

Despite Eve's mammoth efforts, Li insisted that her plans for a low-key, beach wedding will go without a hitch. When Eve and Owen got married, they had the wedding to top all weddings. Their no expense spared luxury affair took no less than three years to plan, so it's understandable that Eve is perplexed at the thought of planning a wedding in just six short days. My only concern is how they'll make a long-distance marriage work, but as Gina rather rudely pointed out, it really isn't any of our business.

Applying a quick slick of lipstick, I fasten Noah into his car seat and check my watch. After a few hours of fun at the turtle sanctuary earlier, it's not just the children who are exhausted. If anything, Oliver, Marc and Owen returned even more worn out than the kids. Glancing over at Oliver who looks like he could drop off at any moment, I give him a gentle prod as a minibus pulls up outside. With everyone being so tired, Eve decided that she would liven us all up with a trip out to her friend's restaurant. Admittedly, no one apart from Eve seemed up for leaving the villa, but now that I am dressed, I'm actually looking forward to sampling some yummy local delicacies.

Stepping out into the warm evening air, I smile at the friendly cab driver and buckle in Noah. My full-length jersey dress clings to my balmy skin as I slide into my seat. The intensity of the heat on the island is something that I didn't expect. The strong midday sun is one thing, but when you open your door at night and feel as though you're walking into an oven, it makes doing anything more than eating and sleeping near impossible. Wiping a bead of sweat from my forehead, I breathe a sigh of relief as the driver starts the engine and fires up the air-conditioning.

'Are we all hungry?' Eve grins spinning around in her seat.

A tiny round of applause rings around the cab as Madison yawns loudly. It looks like Eve is going to have to come up with a little more than rice and peas if she wants to excite this miserable lot. Watching the many trees whizz past the car window, I listen to Madison as she fills us in on her amazing day with the turtles. Eve and Gina are yet to hear about their terrific turtle adventures, but since Oliver returned it is all that he has talked about. Who would have thought that a man of his age would be so impressed with an afternoon spent feeding turtles?

'What did you do today?' Madison asks, grabbing a handful of her black curls and twirling them around her little fingers.

'We planned Auntie Lianna's wedding.' I smile brightly at her as her eyes widen at the word *wedding*.

'Can I be a bridesmaid?' She squeals, clutching her hands to her face. 'Can I be a bridesmaid? Please! Please! Please!'

Gina laughs and ruffles Madison's hair. 'I think that is up to Auntie Lianna.'

Madison's face falls and I don't know whether to tell her or not that Li has already confirmed Madison will indeed be a bridesmaid. Deciding to leave that special moment to the bride-to-be, I unbuckle my seat belt as the minibus comes to a stop outside an open-air restaurant. Leaving Oliver and Owen to settle the bill, I hop onto the pavement and glance around. Considering that it is so early in the evening the place is pretty busy. The pretty wood fronted property is right in the centre of a busy strip, with giant lanterns framing the entrance. Laughter floats out from the many happy customers who are merrily enjoying their evening meal.

Waiting for the rest of our group to sort themselves out, I pass Noah's car seat to Oliver as we make our way inside. Adjusting her frankly fabulous Valentino dress, Eve sashays on ahead to find her friend. Squeezing our way through the cluster of tables, we follow her instructions and take a seat at the bar. Waitresses buzz past us with plates of delicious food and I bite my lip in anticipation.

'Andrea!' Eve squeals, throwing her arms around the neck of an elderly Bajan lady. 'How are you?'

'Very well, my friend.' Andrea smiles warmly and puts her hands on her hips. 'Please, let me show you to your table.' Pushing chairs out of the way, she beckons for us to follow her.

We follow the bar around to the right and out onto the balcony. Blue waters stretch out as far as the eye can see, setting the scene for the perfect, uninterrupted sunset. Sliding into a seat, I place Noah between Oliver and myself and laugh as Gina struggles to get in with her big bum. To say that none of us were really up for coming out tonight was an understatement, but this place really is beautiful. Picking up my menu, I lick my lips as I eye up the many intriguing appetisers.

'What are you having?' I ask Gina, not wanting to order a starter if no one else is.

'Everything!' She scoffs, grabbing a handful of peanuts from the table.

Shaking my head, I try to keep Noah occupied with my phone as the rest of the group order drinks with Andrea. Deciding that I have had enough rum punch to last me a lifetime, I opt for a Diet Coke and look out over the calm water.

'It's such a shame Lianna had to run off.' Eve takes Melrose from Marc and bounces her on her knee. 'We could have toasted the happy couple.'

'It's definitely going ahead then, this wedding?' Owen asks, dabbing a napkin on his forehead.

'It is indeed.' I confirm, twisting my own wedding band around my finger. 'In six short days, Lianna will be a married woman.'

'I've got deja vu.' Marc chuckles as a little laugh goes around the table.

'I know, but this time I think she actually has something with Vernon.' I lock eyes with Marc who eventually nods his head in agreement.

You can't blame Marc for being a little pessimistic. After every one of Lianna's messy breakups, it was Marc and myself who had to pick up the pieces. Although you have to give it to Vernon, he actually seems just as infatuated with Lianna as she does with him. Breathing in the salty sea air, I watch another table clink cocktail glasses together happily and immediately regret my decision to order a soft drink. The restaurant is buzzing with the excitement, but at the same time keeps a laid-back ambience, in the way that only Barbados can. This relaxed pace of life is something that I will miss when we return to the UK. The hustle and bustle of London's cosmopolitan streets seem a million miles away right now.

'So, apart from Lianna's impending nuptials, is there anything else you guys wanna do for the rest of the trip?' Oliver asks, accepting an ice-cold glass of beer from Andrea.

'I want to do a catamaran trip. You know, the one where you can swim with the turtles?' Handing MJ a bottle of water, Gina reaches into her handbag and produces a selection of pamphlets. 'There are actually a few things we could do. Rum tours, surf lessons, scuba diving... oh, and there's a golf club.'

I spot Oliver's eyes light up at the mention of golf.

'Could I see those for a second?' He reaches over and takes the golf leaflet from Gina.

Strategically placing it between himself and Owen, he gives him a little nudge as they both become engrossed in the text. Locking eyes with Eve, I shake my head and turn my attention to the tasty looking menu. Deciding between the chicken and the fish takes me a good five minutes. If it were just Oliver and I, I'm not ashamed to admit that I would have gone for both, but seeing as though we have company, I decide to be a lady and plump for the chicken. Waiting until the rest of them have placed their orders, I take the pile of pamphlets and flick through the pages. If we had the time, I would do each and every one of these. Let's face it, I don't think I have much chance of swimming with turtles back in London. Not unless I put a few in my bathtub with me anyway.

'When did we arrange to go wedding dress shopping with Li?' Gina's brow furrows as she fights with Madison for her lipstick.

'Day after tomorrow.' Eve confirms, licking her lips.

'Please tell me you didn't just say wedding dress shopping?' Oliver runs a hand through his hair and sighs dramatically.

'I'm sure we can give the boys a day pass to enjoy the golf. What do you say, ladies?' Tearing apart a bread roll, I hand a piece to Noah and wait for them to reply.

'I guess so...' Gina muses, devouring a handful of nuts in one giant mouthful. 'But wouldn't you be terribly upset at missing out on hour after hour of trying on bridal gowns?'

'I think we would survive.' Oliver laughs, reaching for his drink.

Taking a sip of my Diet Coke, I giggle as Noah reaches out for more bread.

'What about you, Marc?' Eve asks, handing him the leaflet. 'Are you joining the boys on their little golfing trip?'

'I guess so, but you do know that if we're going down the boy/girl route, the boys can come with us and you can take the girls along to your shopping trip.' Leaning back in his seat, he flashes me a wink and motions to the kids.

'That seems fair enough.' Eve smiles at Madison and pulls her ponytail gently.

I let out a quiet scoff and look over at Gina. Being childless, Eve doesn't really understand just how difficult everyday tasks can be when you throw kids into the mix. Truth be told, I would take Noah and MJ over Madison and Melrose any day. Eve hasn't been exposed to one of Madison's mega meltdowns before, so I don't think she really knows what she is letting herself in for. We have definitely pulled the short straw on this one.

The boys chat animatedly about their impending golf trip as Gina and Eve discuss what kind of wedding dress Li will go for. Turning around in my seat, I watch a young couple walk hand in hand along the shore. Pausing to take photographs of each other, they ask a passer-by to take one of the pair of them and fall about laughing as a couple of locals photobomb them.

The trees rustle behind them as they continue on their journey, creating the perfect background noise to the pretty scene. Exhaling quietly, I pluck Noah from his highchair and plant a kiss on his head. Music starts to play down on the beach and the entire table erupts into laughter as Gina starts to dance in her seat. Accepting another drink from Andrea, I take a sip and join in the laughter.

Looking around the table at everyone's smiling faces, I try to commit the moment to memory. Vernon might have stolen Lianna's heart, but I think it's safe to say that Barbados has taken hold of ours...

Chapter 11

'Are you sure you'll be OK?' I bite my lip anxiously as Eve takes hold of Noah.

'We will be *fine*.' Laughing off my concerns, she tickles Noah on the tummy and turns to face Owen. 'Isn't that right, Owen?'

My eyes flit to Owen as he looks down at Melrose dubiously. Why do I have a feeling that this is not going to be as easy as they think? Over dinner last night, Gina decided that today we would do a catamaran trip. What she didn't realise at the time, was that the kids didn't meet the minimum age requirements to take part. Suddenly deciding that she could do with some practice, Eve jumped in and offered to play mummy for the day. Now, if you don't know Eve you would be forgiven for not finding this unusual, but ever since I met her, she has made it crystal clear that children are *not* on her radar. The fact she has volunteered for an afternoon of chasing around after four excitable children is more than a little out of character.

The sun shines brightly down on us as I hover on the harbour, not knowing whether or not to stay behind.

'Are we going to the beach yet?' Madison asks, jumping up and down on the spot.

'In a minute.' Owen whispers, looking frankly terrified.

Stifling a laugh, I pull my bag up onto my sunburnt shoulder. A few more people have gathered at the pickup point, signalling that it is almost time to leave.

Pushing my sunglasses up into my hair, I let out a sigh plant a kiss on Noah's cheek.

'Clara!' Oliver yells over the music. 'They'll be fine. Let's go!'

'You have all of our numbers if you need anything at all.' Blowing them a kiss, I pause for a moment before squeezing my way through the crowd.

Smiling apologetically at Gina, I take a sip from my water bottle and look over my shoulder. 'I'm really worried about them!'

'About who?' Marc scoffs. 'The Lakes or the kids?'

'Very funny, but I'm being serious! I just hope they can handle it.' I'm trying to stay positive, but my mothering instincts are causing me to fret.

Lianna links her arm through mine and shoots me a wink. 'Don't worry!'

'Trust me, when you have three of them, you will be *thankful* when someone foolishly agrees to take them!' Cackling loudly, Gina adjusts her tiny swimsuit and waves at the cute captain.

Rolling my eyes, I apply a layer of SPF to my lips. I suppose they're right. I mean, what's the worst that could happen? Telling myself not to worry, I try to shake it off and get into the spirit of things. Swimming with turtles has always been something that I have wanted to do. We actually came close in Mexico but opted for a dolphin trip instead. Fiddling with my ticket, I glance at Marc and try to work out what he is up to. As you already know, Marc can't swim, so I am very puzzled as to why he has chosen to come along today. For as long as I have known him, Marc has avoided any situation that could possibly put him in deep water. For him to have a sudden change of heart and voluntarily be taken out to sea to be thrown in with the turtles is more than a little perturbing.

Following the rest of the group onto the boat, I slide onto the bench and get settled to listen to the welcome speech. From what I can gather, we are going to eat, drink, swim with the turtles and then eat and drink some more. Accepting a glass of rum punch, I pull down the straps on my dress as the motor kicks in and we pull away from the harbour. The ocean sparkles like diamonds under the strong rays as we move along the water. Feeling myself start to relax, I enjoy the sensation of the wind in my hair. Other customers clink their plastic cups together happily and pose for photos against the amazing backdrop.

'Isn't this amazing?' Lianna breathes, stretching out in her seat. 'I could *live* on one of these.'

'Some people do...' Vernon muses, whipping off his top and joining her.

'Really?' Struggling with the zipper on my shorts, I finally manage to wiggle out of them and collapse onto the bench with a thud.

'Yeah. They got rum, fish, the open water. What more do you need?' He rubs SPF into his shoulders and chuckles. 'I've often thought about it myself.'

I look around and have to admit that he has got a point. Glancing over at Oliver who is talking animatedly to the crew, I take a sip of my punch and stretch out to enjoy the sunshine. A group of girls opposite have learner plates taped to their t-shirts, signalling to the world that they are on a hen-do.

'Are you having a hen-do?' I ask, rolling over to face Lianna.

'A what?' Vernon laughs.

'She means a bachelorette party.' Li laughs, resting her head on his shoulder.

'Damn straight she's having a bachelorette party!' He slips off his sunglasses and throws an arm around Lianna's shoulders.

'Does that mean you've already planned your stag-do?' I ask, raising my eyebrows in mock horror.

'Bachelor party.' Li translates, entwining her fingers with his.

'What *are* we doing for a stag-do?' Marc chips in, not one to miss out on a party.

'Funnily enough, my brother asked me the same thing.' Vernon shrugs his shoulders as Marc looks at him expectantly. 'I'm just going to leave that to him. I don't want anything crazy though, just a traditional Bajan bachelor party.'

'What exactly does a traditional Bajan bachelor party entail?' Oliver asks, tearing himself away from the friendly instructor.

'A little fishing, some rum, dominoes, a cigar or two...' Vernon pushes himself to his feet and leans over the railing. 'You guys up for that?'

Oliver's face lights up at the prospect of fishing and they immediately begin discussing their plans. Taking the opportunity to quiz Li about her own hen-do, I accept a refill on my punch and turn to face her.

'So, that's Vernon's sorted, what are we doing for yours?

'Can we get a stripper?' Gina's eyes gleam as she rubs tanning oil into her already brown legs.

'I don't think so...' Lianna wags a finger and looks at us sternly. 'I don't want anything stupid.'

Locking eyes with Gina, I flash her a knowing wink. We both know that Lianna would love a crazy hen-do. This, *I don't want any fuss* protest is all an act. Deciding to leave it for now, I roll onto my side and watch the boys chat happily. Boats have never really been my thing, but this is strangely relaxing. All this bobbing around would normally make me seasick. Today, however, couldn't be more different. With the sun shining down on me and the wind in my hair, I couldn't feel more at ease.

Noticing that the boys are out of earshot, I slide over to Gina and point at Marc. 'What's going on there?' I ask, chewing on the end of my straw.

'What do you mean?' Shielding her eyes from the sun, she rocks her shoulders in time to the music.

'Marc hates water.' I whisper, pushing my sunglasses up into my hair.

Pursing her lips, Gina raises her eyebrows innocently. 'I don't know.'

I squint my eyes suspiciously as she rolls onto her stomach. 'Yes, you do! What's going on?'

'Nothing!' She protests, holding up her hands in defence.

'Gina!' Slapping her on the bum, I take her beaker and refuse to give it back until she fesses up.

'Alright!' Shuffling into a sitting position, she snatches back her drink and lowers her voice to little more than a whisper. 'James has been teaching Marc how to swim.'

'What?' My brow creases into a frown. 'James the chef?'

'Yes, James the chef.' Glancing over her shoulder to make sure that no one is listening, she motions for me to keep my voice down.

'That's amazing! So, can he swim now?' I look over at Marc and feel a swell of pride.

Shrugging her shoulders in response, she finishes her drink and pushes herself to her feet. 'I honestly don't know. I didn't want to pressure him by bugging him about it.'

Taking that as my cue to shut up, I reach over for my bag and pull out my sun cream. I notice a faint tan line on my shoulders and feel a wave of excitement. I am going to catch a tan on this holiday if it kills me.

Eyeing up Oliver's brown back enviously, I stand to attention as the boat comes to a sudden stop. Watching the instructor throw the anchor overboard, I sneak a peek at Marc. Laughing heartily, he takes a life jacket from the pile and slips it over his head. I don't quite believe what I'm seeing here. If he gets in there and starts whirling around like Nemo I am going to die.

'Alright!' The instructor claps his hands together to get everyone's attention and smiles brightly. 'As most of you now know, my name is Lucas and I will be your instructor for the day.'

A little cheer echoes around the catamaran as we get ready for the main event. Lucas instructs us to all to put on our life jackets and hands out snorkelling equipment. Looking rather smug, Oliver declines and pulls out his own snorkel mask. Unlike the green plastic pieces that Lucas is handing out, Oliver's is striking silver with chrome edges. Quietly wishing that I had also bought one, I tug on my mask and join the queue. As Lucas helps a young girl down the steps, a couple behind us decide to dive straight in off the edge of the boat. I lock eyes with Lianna as she smiles and tugs on her mask.

'Where are you going?' Gina asks, tearing herself away from her cocktail.

Tightening the straps on her bikini, Lianna positions herself on the edge of the boat before jumping straight into the sea. Before I have the chance to join her, another three bodies crash in beside her. Letting out a laugh when I realise that the other bodies belong to Oliver, Vernon and Gina, I am about to dive in after them when I spot Marc hovering by the steps.

'Are you getting in?' I ask casually, not wanting to put any pressure on him.

'Thinking about it...' He smiles uneasily and fiddles with his mask.

Returning his smile, I squeeze past him and make my way into the water. A few people let out squeals as a turtle fires past us. Kicking my legs, I swim over to the others and discreetly watch Marc out of the corner of my eye. Dipping his toe into the water, he takes a couple of steps forward before retreating back onto the boat. *Come on, Marc!* Mentally cheering him on, I bite my lip as he adjusts his mask and slowly makes his way down the steps. *Just two more steps!* I am about to nudge Gina when I realise that they are all watching, too.

Pausing on the final step, he seems to contemplate his next move for an eternity before falling back into the ocean. *He did it! I can't believe that he is actually in the water!* Splashing around like a lost dolphin, he splutters and coughs for a moment before doggy-paddling over to us. To anyone else, he will surely look ridiculous, but I couldn't be prouder. Yes, he has a life vest on and therefore couldn't drown if he tried, but this is a huge achievement for him. I am about to let out an almighty cheer when Gina grabs my hand and shakes her head.

'He won't want the attention.' She whispers, holding out her arms as he comes to a stop beside her. 'Well done!'

Resisting the urge to squeal, I smile brightly and give him a congratulatory high five. Lucas beckons us over to hand feed the turtles and I follow the crowd like a happy fish. The turtles were supposed to be the main attraction, but seeing Marc face his fears like this has really made my day. A thirty-something making a splash in a life jacket might not be the biggest triumph in history, but I am a big believer in that all achievements should be celebrated. After all, every accomplishment both large and small starts with the same decision to try...

Chapter 12

'Can you believe that Marc actually got into the water yesterday?' Li asks, holding the frankly horrible garment against her body.

'Don't change the subject.' Snatching the offending dress out of her hands, Gina slams it back onto the rail. 'I wouldn't be any kind of friend to you if I let you get married in *that*.'

'You don't look like a princess.' Madison mumbles, shaking her head and sticking out her tongue. 'I don't like it.'

Sighing dramatically, Lianna folds her arms and pushes her way out onto the street. 'How many times have I got to tell you all that I don't *care* what I wear. It's not about the dress.'

I scratch my nose in a poor attempt to cover a yawn. 'You *do* care, Li. You know you do.'

'You do care! You do care!' Madison chants, pointing at Lianna and giggling like a Gremlin.

'What about Vernon?' Gina pushes. 'I'm sure he doesn't want to see you walking down the aisle in a cheap, cotton maxi dress.'

'Well, I think Vernon would marry you in a bin liner.' Smiling sweetly, Eve takes Madison's hand and shoots Lianna a wink.

Li rolls her eyes as we walk along in the sunshine. Taking Melrose's pram to give Gina a break, I pause to tie up my hair. Before today I didn't think it was possible to tire of retail therapy, but after half a day of shopping with two girls under five, I am starting to question my beliefs. For the past three hours, we have been scouring the shops in a desperate bid to find a wedding dress for Li. As soon as we left the villa this morning, Lianna made it quite clear that she didn't want a traditional wedding dress and if we don't find anything soon, she is going to get her wish.

Taking a sip of her water, Gina shields the sun from her eyes and pauses to look around. We must have been in over thirty shops and we haven't come across anything even close to being wedding appropriate. Unless Li wants to say *I do* in a flimsy kaftan she'd better find something, and she'd better find it fast.

'Let's look in here.' I point to a rustic looking store on the other side of the road. 'If there's nothing in there then we're going to have to go back to the villa.'

'I want to go back villa!' Madison screams, jumping up and down and turning red in the face.

'Let's just try this last one.' I offer her a tired smile which she returns with a frown.

Not waiting for us to catch up, Lianna crosses the street and pushes her way inside. Deliberately staying a few steps behind, I tug Gina's sleeve and pull her closer.

'What are we going to do with her?' I whisper, tucking a stray strand of hair behind my ear. 'I know that she's going for the whole laid-back Caribbean vibe, but not having a proper wedding dress? She will regret it. I know she will.'

'Maybe she really doesn't care what she wears.' Eve muses. 'I think it's incredibly romantic.'

'Well, I think it's stupid.' Letting out a scoff, Gina looks both ways before dragging us across the street.

Taking off my sunglasses, I slip into the shop and exhale gratefully as the ice-cold air-conditioning cools my warm skin instantly. Glad to be out of the strong sun, I run my eyes over the rails of dresses and try to pick out anything white. From beach dresses to simple kaftans, there seems to be everything you could ever want in here, except a wedding dress.

Gina plucks out a strapless jersey dress and frowns before pushing it back into the pile. 'How hard can it be to find a bloody wedding dress?'

'Probably not very hard if you're looking in an actual wedding dress shop.' I yell as loudly as possible in order to ensure that Li can hear me.

For some reason, Lianna has refused to visit a wedding dress shop. Why? I have no idea. Flicking through a rail of wrap dresses, I bite the inside of my cheek and start to feel a little concerned. My best friend is getting married in a matter of days and she doesn't have a wedding dress. Personally, I don't know how she isn't having a full-scale meltdown.

'What about this one?' Li's voice pierces my thought bubble as I wander over to see what she has picked out.

I shake my head and rub my throbbing temples as she shoves it back onto the rail. Melrose lets out a whimper and I rock her pram gently. Please don't wake up. The last thing we need is a screaming baby on our hands. Diving back into the dresses, Li pulls out up a white satin maxi dress and holds it against her.

A store assistant nods in approval and slips out from behind the till. 'Very pretty and you've certainly got the figure for it.'

'She has, but it's for a wedding...' I mumble enviously, taking a glimpse of her name badge. Delores, what a lovely name.

'This is *great* for a wedding!' Smiling brightly, Delores takes another dress from the rail and holds it up. 'We also have this one. This colour will look great on you.'

Giving the magenta skater dress a quick glance, I shake my head and take the white dress from Lianna. 'It's for a wedding, so it has to be white.'

'White?' Delores clasps her hands to her face in horror. 'Oh, no! Only the *bride* should wear white.'

'She *is* the bride!' Eve giggles, leading Madison away from an intricate jewellery display.

Delores looks back and forth between the both us, an alarmed expression on her face. '*You're* the bride?'

'I certainly am.' Lianna smiles proudly and holds out her enormous ring.

Delores whips her glasses off her head and plants them on the bridge of her nose.

'Please tell her that she's crazy!' Gina interrupts crudely. 'She can't get married without a wedding dress, she just can't!'

'Your friend is right! You *can't* get married without a decent dress.' Motioning for us to follow her, she pushes her way through the rails into the back of the store. 'That ring needs a dress that is *equally* as special.'

Flashing Gina a confused look, I shrug my shoulders and hope for the best. As we snake through the small shop, I catch Lianna eyeing up a white wrap dress and slap her hands away. Shooting her the sternest stare that I can muster, I bite my lip as we come to a store cupboard. With a quick wink, Delores disappears inside, leaving the six of us standing around like a pack of lost puppies.

'This was a stupid idea.' Gina whispers angrily. 'We should have bitten the bullet and gone straight for the wedding dress shops.'

I am about to retort that this was actually *her* idea when the store cupboard door sweeps open. Smiling excitedly, Delores holds out a selection of dress bags. The top one is covered in dust and the others don't look like they have seen sunlight in years. Feeling deflated, I smile uneasily at Delores as she ushers us into the changing rooms. Lianna pinches my arm and I know without looking at her that she wants to run in the opposite direction. Not wanting to be rude, I take a seat on an old sofa and pay attention as Delores unzips the first bag. It's certainly a lot more formal than anything else that we have seen today. The timeless, ivory, shift dress screams Hollywood glamour, but it's not exactly what I would call a wedding dress.

'It's fab!' Gina squeals, pushing Lianna forward. 'Try it on!'

'Do you like it?' Eve asks, shooting the dress a quick glance. 'Is that the kind of thing you were thinking of?'

Lianna takes the dress and runs her fingers over the fabric. 'I'm not sure.'

'Just try it!' Delores begs, holding out the dress. 'You can't be sure until you try it.'

Watching Lianna slip behind the curtain, I usher Gina in behind her to help with the zip. A quick glance at my watch tells me that we have just a few hours of sunlight left. I sincerely hope that Delores has something special hidden in one of these bags or Lianna is going to be getting married in a white beach towel. Hearing the distinct sound of a zipper being pulled, I look up as Gina pulls back the curtain.

'It's gorgeous!' I breathe, motioning for her to spin around. 'I just don't think it says *bride*...'

'I agree.' Reaching out and picking a piece of cotton off the hem, Gina shakes her head and yawns. 'Next one.'

Delores frowns at our dismissive comments and reaches for the next bag. 'Well, I like it.'

'Me, too.' Eve gushes. 'It's really... unique.'

I look at Lianna for her opinion, but she simply shrugs her shoulders. 'I don't mind it.'

'But do you *love* it?' Gina presses, leaning against the railing. 'You are supposed to *love* your wedding dress.'

Shaking her head, she rolls her eyes and retreats back into the changing room. Mentally kicking myself for criticising the one dress that could possibly pass as acceptable, I fix a smile to my face as Delores takes the second dress from the bag.

'Now *that* is a wedding dress.' My eyes sparkle as the soft chiffon shines under the bright lights.

'This definitely says beach wedding!' Gina claps her hands together excitedly and takes the knee length gown off the hanger.

Crossing my fingers that this is the one, I watch with bated breath as Gina hands the dress through the curtain to Lianna.

Unlike the hundreds of other dresses that we have dismissed today, this one is exactly what I would have picked out for her. Dainty, simple, floaty and flirty. What more could you possibly want from a wedding dress?

'I think this is the one!' I whisper to Madison as she gives me the thumbs-up sign.

Suddenly feeling extremely optimistic, I sit back in my seat and feel myself start to relax. Maybe today won't turn out to be a disaster after all. Tugging Madison onto my knee, I cover her eyes as we wait for the big reveal.

I hear undefined mumbling from behind the curtain and find myself straining my ears to hear what is going on.

'It's perfect!' Gina gasps. 'I love it!'

'It is?' I yell, a little too loudly considering that we are in an enclosed space.

'Let me see!' Madison screeches, tearing my hands away from her eyes.

Squealing in anticipation, I jump up and throw back the curtain. With a delicate scooped neckline and an empire waist, it is so simple yet beautifully elegant. Gina's right, it's absolutely perfect. It couldn't *be* more perfect.

'Li! You look like an angel!' I clasp my hands to my face and try to stop the tears from falling. 'It's beautiful.'

'Incredible.' Eve confirms, wiping away a stray tear.

Spinning around to Delores, I throw my arms around her and breathe a sigh of relief. 'You are a lifesaver.'

Shaking off my praise, she takes a handful of flowers from the vase in the window and shakes off the water before handing them to Lianna. My heart pangs as she holds the flowers in front of her like a bouquet. *Now* she looks like a bride. Madison's cheeks turn pink and I know by her silence that we have her seal of approval, too. High-fiving Gina and Eve, I am about to breathe a sigh of relief when Lianna speaks up.

'I don't know...' She mumbles, clearly not very impressed.

Feeling shell-shocked, my mouth drops open as we all turn around to face her.

'What do you mean?' I ask, my brow creasing into a frown.

Looking at her reflection in the mirror, she scrunches up her nose and shrugs her shoulders. 'I don't like it.' She shakes her head and motions for me to unzip her.

'What do you mean you don't like it?' Gina yells furiously. 'It's stunning!'

'It's perfect!' Delores chips in, obviously as perturbed as the rest of us.

I wait for Lianna to explain further, but she just sticks out her bottom lip and sighs.

'Wait a minute, I thought you didn't care what you got married in?' Folding her arms, Gina squints her eyes at Lianna and taps her foot impatiently.

Ignoring our protests, Li looks down at the dress doubtfully. 'Well, maybe I do.'

Not knowing whether to laugh or cry, I lock eyes with Gina and shake my head.

'Sorry, Delores. I really appreciate all your help.' Attempting a small smile, Lianna hands her back the flowers and looks down at her feet.

'Aren't you going to try the last one?' Eve points to the last bag on the rail hopefully.

'Try it!' Madison demands, stamping her feet in annoyance.

Giving in to the peer pressure, she asks Gina to unzip her and takes the bag into the changing room.

'It might be a little big, but don't worry. I can sort that for you.' Delores pushes her glasses up the bridge of her nose and smiles broadly as a customer walks into the shop.

We wait in silence for a moment, before Lianna finally speaks up. 'I'll take it.'

'Really?' I attempt to slip inside the changing room, but Lianna holds the curtain firmly closed.

'No!' She yells loudly. 'I don't want you to see it.'

'Why?' I shoot Gina a confused look as we both stand behind the curtain, ready to pounce the second that she lets go.

'Because you're just going to say that you don't like it, and this is one that I actually *do* like...'

Her voice is so small that I suddenly feel a little bad. At the end of the day, it's Lianna's choice what she wears at her own wedding. Have I crossed the line from helpful friend to over-bearing control freak? Picking up Madison, I ignore the glares that I am getting from Eve.

'We won't, Li. I promise.'

Holding onto the curtain, she pokes her head out and squints her eyes. 'I don't believe you.'

'We'll be nice. Won't we, Gina?' I poke Gina in the ribs and nod furiously.

Gina holds her hands in the air and smiles. 'Cross my heart.'

'I'll keep them in check, Li. Don't you worry.' Taking control of the situation, Eve smiles confidently and motions for her to come out.

Holding my breath, I bite my lip as Lianna draws back the curtain. Not knowing what to say, I resort to a silent gasp as she twirls around. Gina's jaw drops open as she nods in approval. Despite our obvious appreciation for the frankly incredible dress, no one says a word.

'Well?' Li probes, resting her hands on her hips. 'What do you think?'

'I love it.' Gina gushes. 'It's not what I thought you would want, but I do love it.'

'Princess!' Madison screams with delight and throws herself at Lianna.

My eyes scan the dress, taking in each and every detail. The beaded fishtail gown hugs every curve and the plunging neckline makes her look even more statuesque than she usually does. The crisp white fabric looks striking against her golden skin, making it obvious to the world that she is most definitely the bride.

'I love it, too.' I sigh, eyeing up the stunning gown. 'You look absolutely incredible. It's flawless.'

'Flawless.' Eve confirms, practically drooling over the beautiful gown.

'Well, it's not quite flawless.' Spinning around, she points to the waist and pulls out a handful of fabric. 'It's a few inches too big.'

Trying not to feel envious that a dress so small could possibly be big, I look at Delores for help.

'I can deal with that.' She trills, smiling widely. 'Let me get my tape measure.'

Watching her whizz off through the shop, I push myself to my feet and throw my arms around Lianna. 'You're going to be the most beautiful bride the world has ever seen.'

A lump forms in my throat as I look at my best friend. I can't believe that she is the same girl who flew out of the UK just a matter of days ago. All the stresses of Periwinkle seem to have melted away and in their place is a chilled, loved-up Li. My head might be asking a million and one questions about how she is going to make this marriage work when there are over four thousand miles between them, but my heart is willing her to take a chance and go for it. I guess it really is true love when you genuinely don't care what you walk down the aisle in. It's obvious to anyone that Lianna isn't doing this for the wedding, she is doing it for love. Mad, crazy, can't be without each other love.

Wiping away a stray tear, I step to the side as Delores returns with a sewing kit the size of Mount Kilimanjaro. Fluffing up her afro, she instructs Lianna to stand still and gets to work at pinning the dress to fit her body. Humming away happily as she transforms the dress into a second skin, Delores pats Li on the bum as she puts in the final pin. Standing back to see the final effect, Lianna lets out a squeal and twirls around like a little girl.

'Now it's flawless!' Gina breathes, nodding in approval.

'How soon can the alterations be done?' I ask, bringing us back to reality with a bump. 'The wedding is in four days...'

I watch Delores screw up her nose and reach into her pocket for a little red notepad. 'It's going to be tough, but I think I can make it work.'

A round of applause echoes around our group as Lianna throws herself at Delores gratefully.

'You, Delores, are a superstar!' Planting a kiss on her cheek, I rub my tired eyes. 'Seriously, you have well and truly saved the day.'

Brushing off our compliments Delores rushes off to serve a customer, leaving the three of us to talk.

'Happy now?' I ask, helping her out of the frankly fabulous gown.

'Very happy.' With a final glance at her reflection, she shuffles into the changing room and pulls the curtain behind her.

'Now that we have found you a dress, can we *please* go for a cocktail?' Gina crosses her fingers as she waits for a response.

'I sincerely hope that you haven't had enough?' Lianna throws back the curtain and hands me the dress bag.

'What do you mean?' Gina and I ask in unison, my head throbbing at the thought of yet more shopping.

'Well, now that we have got *my* dress sorted, we just need to buy *yours*...'

Chapter 13

'Well?' I ask, spinning around in my newly acquired bridesmaid dress. 'What do you think?'

Oliver looks up from the television briefly and nods. 'Fantastic.'

'Is that it?' I retort in annoyance. 'Seven hours of shopping, a thousand dresses and all you can say is *fantastic*.'

'It's beautiful, babe. Perfect.' He pulls me down for a kiss before returning to his football match.

Resisting the urge to turn the damn thing off, I wander into the bathroom and check out my reflection in the huge floor to ceiling mirror. After the draining search for Lianna's dress, it took us a further two hours to find bridesmaid dresses that we all agreed on. Strangely, for a bride who wasn't bothered about what she wore, she had some very strict stipulations on what she wanted us to wear.

Looking at the striking blue dress, I have to admit that it isn't as bad as it could have been. At one point, we nearly gave in and agreed to wear a lime green strapless piece. I think the combination of heat and exhaustion was severely affecting our judgement.

Shimmying out of the dress, I place it on a hanger and wander back into the bedroom. Whilst the girls were out trawling the shops, the boys took to the golf course and I have to admit that they returned even more exhausted than us. Although I still find it hard to understand what is fun about chasing a ball around in the strong Caribbean sun, they do look like they had a fantastic time. Dropping down onto the bed, I take a peek into Noah's cot and smile as I watch his little chest rise and fall.

After all the chaos of the past few days, I am really looking forward to tonight. As usual, Lianna has flounced off to The Hangout and the Strokers have joined Owen and Eve for a meal out at the local fish fry. Deciding to give the activities a miss, Oliver and I opted for a night in with Noah and pizza, just the three of us. Football, however, was not on the agenda.

'Can you turn that off now?' I grumble, reaching over and taking another slice even though I am already fit for bursting. 'I was promised a romantic night in.'

Muttering something under his breath, he reluctantly reaches for the remote and jabs at the off button before crashing back onto the pillows.

'You burnt your nose today.' I grab some moisturiser from the bedside table and squirt a dollop onto the tip of his nose. 'You should be more careful.'

Rolling his eyes, he makes a grab for the last slice and chews with his eyes closed. I think it's safe to say that he is as pooped as I am. All this fun in the sun seems to have taken its toll. Drinking cocktails, snorkelling and eating yummy food all day isn't as easy as it looks, you know.

'Marc mentioned that Vernon joined you guys earlier?' Rolling onto my side, I prop myself up on the pillows.

He nods in response and pushes himself onto his elbows. 'Yeah. Dude has got it bad.'

'What do you mean?' I ask, with a mouthful of pizza.

'All he talked about all day was Li.' Oliver shakes his head and laughs. 'Lianna, Lianna, Lianna. He's a good guy though. I like him.'

I chew thoughtfully for a moment, letting Oliver's praise sink in. I am about to confess that I like him, too when Oliver starts to speak.

'He was even talking about moving to the UK.'

Shooting him a frown, I hurriedly swallow my pizza and reach for a napkin. 'What did he say, exactly?'

'Exactly that. Marc and I have offered to help with the move if he decides to go for it.'

I lick my lips in a frantic bid to digest this new piece of information. 'What does Lianna have to say about this?'

'Well, I guess she's all for it seeing as though she's marrying the guy.'

Hitting him on the thigh, I toss my pizza crust back into the box. 'I suppose it does make sense.'

'He also mentioned the possibility of Li moving out here...'

'No!' I yell, horrified at the thought of losing my best friend. 'Lianna could never move out of here. She has a business.'

'Vernon has a business, too...'

Choosing to ignore him, I reach for my water and stroll out onto the balcony. Dropping down onto the lounger, I lay back and close my eyes as the sound of crickets chirping surrounds me. Lianna can't move out here, she just can't. Looking up at the black sky above me, I find myself picturing my life without Lianna in it. Don't get me wrong, Lianna and I aren't joined at the hip. In fact, over the past few years, we have actually become rather independent from one other. It's hard to believe that we are the same two girls who would stumble home with a kebab after one too many tequilas. Looking back on the history of our friendship, we couldn't have become more different from the girls that we once were, although through it all we have become closer than ever. Lianna isn't just my friend, she's my sister.

Allowing my eyes to close, I listen to the waves crashing against the shore as a smile plays at the corner of my lips. From dating disasters to fashion faux pas, Li and I have tackled almost everything together. For years now, Oliver and I have wanted Lianna to find a nice man and settle down. We just didn't plan on her settling down thousands of miles away. Why couldn't she have fallen in love with a British man? There are tons of good looking, rich, eligible men in London, only Lianna could agree to marry a man from bloody Barbados.

The unmistakeable sound of Oliver snoring drifts out of the bedroom and I find myself weighing up the pros and cons of living in London and Barbados. On one hand, you have arguably the most cosmopolitan city in the world, filled with bustling bars, revered restaurants and high-end hotels. On the other, you have Barbados, idyllic beaches, sunny weather and a laid-back lifestyle that most city workers would kill for. I know which one I would choose if I were her, although it's not my decision, is it?

Pushing myself to my feet, I take a final glance at the glistening black water before heading back inside. The heat from outside has gotten the better of the air-conditioning, resulting in a very sweaty Oliver crashed out in a pizza induced coma. Deciding to leave him, I clear away the remnants of our dinner and check on Noah before crawling in beside him. My usually pale skin has acquired a rather lovely golden glow over the past few days, even my deathly pasty legs have managed to catch a little colour. Reaching over and flicking off the light, I stretch out on the incredibly soft sheets and allow my eyes to close. The next few days are going to change Lianna's future forever. I just hope they change it for the best...

* * *

'Good morning!' Flashing James a megawatt smile, I slide Noah into a highchair and reach for the water jug. 'Where is everyone?' Motioning outside, James hands Noah some chunks of cheese and gets back to his frying station.

'Could you watch him for a moment? Oliver will be down in a minute.'

Nodding in response, James plays peekaboo with Noah and turns up the radio. Smiling at the two of them laughing, I flash James a grateful wink and slip outside. The sun blares through the patio windows, lighting up the veranda in a blinding white light. Shielding my eyes from the sun, I wander across the decking and smile.

'What are you doing out here?' I ask, leaning on the back of Marc's chair.

'We were just discussing what we should do today.' Eve sighs, running her fingers through her blonde bob.

'I want to go to the beach!' Madison screams, running across the decking and pointing at the ocean with her chubby fingers.

'I could think of worse ways to spend the day.' Marc mumbles, bouncing Melrose on his knee.

Owen looks up from his paper and raises his eyebrows. 'Sounds good to me.'

'Me too.' I let out a yawn and kick a ball back over to MJ.

'Breakfast is ready.' Oliver hollers from inside, causing MJ to abandon his ball and make a run for the bacon. Like father like son.

Following suit, Madison wriggles out of Gina's arms and tries to beat her brother to the post.

'You not hungry?' I ask Owen, who obviously has no intention of moving from his seat. Shaking his head in response, he rubs his stomach and sighs dramatically.

'I'm still full from last night.'

Flashing him a smile, I follow the others inside and pause by the door. 'Are you sure we can't tempt you? Breakfast is the most important meal of the day...'

Madison screams loudly, demanding more bacon than MJ. Catching Owen's smile falter, I suppress a giggle and leave him to read his paper. Something tells me that his loss of appetite has more to do with a mouthy Madison.

Sliding onto a stool, I take a back seat as Eve starts to roll off an itinerary for the day. In true Eve fashion, everything has to be planned like a military operation. Accepting an omelette from James, I sprinkle it with pepper before picking up my fork and diving in. This is what I will miss the most when we return home. Having a hunky man to cook all our meals is something I could most definitely get used to. Not that I would change Oliver, of course, but my husband's cooking skills don't stretch further than a greasy fry up.

'Can we walk around the bay today?' Gina asks with a mouthful of bacon. 'I want to try parasailing.'

I lock eyes with Oliver and shake my head. I have tried parasailing once before and it did not end well. Reaching for the water as the heat from my omelette starts to grow in the back of my throat, I shake my head at Gina as she tried to bag a parasailing partner.

'How about you?' Pointing her finger at Eve, she leans over and cuts up MJ's bacon into tiny pieces.

'I'm not great with heights...' Flashing her an apologetic smile, Eve tucks into her smoothie.

Only Eve could stick to a low carb, high protein diet whilst everyone else is devouring delicious greasy goodness.

'I'll do it with you.' Chomping on her sausages, Madison dunks a hash brown into a mound of sauce.

'I think you're a little young.' Gina laughs and plants a kiss on Madison's head. 'But you can help me pick who's going to join me.'

Dropping her fork with a clatter, Madison squints her eyes and looks around the table.

'So, which one is it going to be?'

* * *

'Are you ready?' I ask, watching a bead of sweat crawl down Owen's brow. 'I have done it before and it's not that bad. I promise.'

'Didn't you throw up mid-air?' He groans, shielding his eyes from the sun to watch another couple set off on the speed boat.

'Well, yes, but...' I am about to say that was because I had a lot to drink that day when I notice the rum punch in his hand.

My words drift off into inaudible mumbles as Gina beckons him over.

'You will be fine.' Rubbing his arm encouragingly, I give him a friendly nudge as he takes a deep breath and makes his way over to Gina.

Watching him walk away, I bite my lip to stop myself from laughing and pad across the hot sand. After much deliberation, Madison decided that Owen would be the lucky one to accompany her mother on her adrenaline trip. He did try to protest, but at the end of the day, how do you say *no* to a little girl?

'How was he?' Eve asks, rubbing sun cream into MJ's shoulders.

'A little nervous, I have to admit, but he will be fine.' Jumping onto my sun lounger, I pull the parasol over Noah's playpen and hand Oliver a bottle of water.

'Noah smells.' Madison squeals, holding her nose and running over to Marc.

'I think you will find it's your turn.' I mumble to Oliver, taking a magazine from Gina's pile. 'I have done at *least* the last ten.'

Dusting the sand off his chest, he tugs on a t-shirt and plucks up Noah.

'Do you want to do Melrose whilst you're there?' Marc asks hopefully, holding up the wriggling baby.

'I don't think so...' Oliver laughs and grabs the changing bag before reaching for his sunglasses.

Blowing him a kiss, I watch him head off in search of the changing rooms. With the sun on his shoulders and his chocolate curls blowing in the sea breeze, he looks just as gorgeous as the day that I met him. A few bikini-clad women stop him to coo over Noah and I feel my heart swell with pride.

'I think I'll go and see if he needs a hand...' Obviously jealous of the female attention, Marc scoops up Melrose and motions for MJ and Madison to follow him.

'Doesn't that bother you?' Eve asks, frowning at the growing crowd of women.

Popping on my sunglasses, I shake my head and stretch out on my lounger. 'Not at all, as long as they keep their hands to themselves, I couldn't care less.'

'That's what Lianna said.' She mumbles, examining her glossy manicure.

'Lianna?' I scrunch up my nose and watch Oliver disappear into the crowd.

Nodding in response she rolls onto her side and takes a sip of her drink. 'You should see how women throw themselves at Vernon in The Hangout. As soon as they hear that he owns the place, they are all over him like a rash.'

A wave of concern washes over me as I put down my magazine. 'I guess that's the same the world over though, isn't it?'

'I'm afraid it does come with the territory.' She sighs and pulls down her bikini straps.

'Speaking of Lianna, shouldn't she be here by now?' I squint my eyes and attempt to see the face of my watch.

Shaking her head, she sprays tanning oil onto her legs. 'She texted whilst you were with Owen. There's been a problem at the bar. Something to do with a shellfish allergy.' Eve raises her eyebrows and flops back down. 'Apparently, it was pretty bad.'

Scrunching up my nose, I recall the other issues that have happened at The Hangout over the past few days. 'Does The Hangout always have so many problems?'

'What do you mean?'

'Well, first there was a mix-up with the kitchen supplies, then there was that problem with a VIP client and now this?'

'Now that you mention it, I guess it has been a little *injury prone* lately.'

A beach seller stops at our loungers and we politely decline. Wishing that I had Oliver's wallet with me, I lift my glasses for a peek at his jewellery before he leaves. Watching him move along to another beach bum, I twist my wedding band around my finger.

'I thought Vernon hired Stephanie to stop stuff like this from happening?'

'Well, I guess he did, but running a popular beach restaurant isn't as easy as it looks from the other side of the bar.'

'Mmm. I guess...'

Rolling onto my stomach, I twist my knotted hair up into a messy bun and stare out at the water. The hot sun shines down onto my shoulders as my eyelids start to become heavy. Part of me thinks that Lianna would be crazy to turn down the opportunity of a life here in beautiful Barbados. Who needs a thriving business and a flash car when you have the sun, the sand and a drink your hand? After all, that's what money is for, isn't it?'

'I can't wait for Lianna's hen-do.' Eve sighs, ignoring the admiring glances from passers-by. 'I have planned it down to the very last detail.'

I flash her a smile as she starts to reel off the details. Truth be told, I am a little bit gutted that I didn't get to be the one to plan Lianna's last night of freedom. Being her best friend, it kind of comes with the territory, but the fact that I don't know Barbados brought my plans to a swift halt. Thankfully, Eve stepped in and took control of the situation, meaning that Lianna will have the send-off into married life that she deserves.

'It sounds fabulous.' I gush, totally confident that Li will love it.

A champagne breakfast courtesy of James followed by a beach-front massage and an overnight stay at an exclusive five-star resort. I couldn't have planned it better myself.

'I wonder what the boys have in store for Vernon?' I ask, secretly hoping that he gets tied to a lamppost.

'I'm sure we will find out tomorrow.' She mumbles, stretching out her lithe arms above her head.

'Oh, yes.' I mumble, suddenly remembering that we have been invited to The Hangout to meet Vernon's family.

'Have you ever met any of his family?' I ask, spotting Oliver and Marc making their way back over to us, minus the bevy of beauties.

'I can't say that I have, but I'm sure they will be as lovely as Vernon.'

To be honest, I hadn't thought about Vernon's family in all of this. My main concern has been Lianna and what *we* think about the whole affair. I hadn't stopped to consider the fact that he will have friends and family who will probably be just as worried as we are.

Oliver appears at the foot of my sun lounger and hands me a freshly changed Noah. Smothering him in SPF 50, I straighten his little cap and smile. The older he gets, the more he looks like his father. Any slight trace of me in there has completely vanished and all that is left is a mini Oliver. I am about to put him into his playpen when Eve leans over and holds out her arms.

'Let me have a squeeze.' Taking Noah, she plants a kiss on his cheek before settling down on the sand.

I lock eyes with Oliver and try not to smile. For someone who has been adamant that she doesn't want children, Eve has taken quite a shine to the kids on this holiday. From braiding Madison's hair to building sandcastles and playing hide and seek with MJ, she really has been playing the part of doting auntie very well. Taking the opportunity to escape for five minutes, I push myself to my feet.

'Fancy a dip, husband?' Throwing my sunglasses onto the sun lounger, I motion to the water and flash Oliver a smile.

'I guess I could give you five minutes before my wife gets back. I must warn you though, she doesn't take kindly to young, hot British women hitting on me.'

Playfully slapping him on the arm, we walk hand in hand across the beach. The waves crash against the sand as a few teenagers chase after each other along the shoreline. Wading into the warm water, I let Oliver lead the way and slip my shoulders under the surface of the sea. The ocean shimmers like glass all around us and I look down to see hundreds of tiny fish darting around happily. Dipping my head back into the water, I watch Oliver float on his back as the strong waves pull him along.

Swimming over to him, I shake the salty seawater out of my eyes and wrap my arms around his neck. Pushing his hair out of his face, I rub my nose against his and pull him closer with my legs. A speed boat shoots by in the distance, causing a cheer to erupt from the people on the beach. Looking up at the sky, I squint my eyes at the parasailers and try to work out which one is Owen.

'If you're looking for Gina and Owen, they were on that one right there.' Pointing in the opposite direction to where I have been looking, Oliver grabs my legs and dips me back into the water.

Letting out a squeal, I splash around like a drowning cat until I finally regain my footing. Not wanting to go down without a fight, I dive under the water and make a grab for his shorts. Realising that I don't have a chance, I hold my hands up to surrender as he scoops me up into a ball.

'Go on then, Mrs Morgan. You know you want to.'

Smiling wickedly, I wiggle out of his grip and dunk his head beneath the water. Squealing with delight, I stick my tongue out as he comes up for air.

The sun glares down on us as I float into his arms and plant a kiss onto his nose. 'And that, Oliver Morgan, is why I married you...'

Chapter 14

Wiping a tear from my eye, I clutch my throbbing stomach and will myself to stop laughing. My sides are aching and my cheeks are actually sore. Holding up my hands in protest, I beg Gina to stop talking. Catching Owen's eye, I find myself feeling a little sorry for him. For the past thirty minutes, Gina has been giving us the lowdown on her parasailing adventure with Owen.

'Stop!' I plead, shaking my head. 'You're killing me.'

'Yeah, stop!' Eve giggles, wrapping an arm around Owen's neck. 'I think he has suffered enough for one day.'

Finally relenting, Gina turns her attention back to her rum punch as a small cry comes out of the baby monitor. Chewing on the end of my straw, I am about to go and check on the kids when Eve jumps to her feet.

'I'll go.' Smiling sweetly, she slips on her sandals and quickly jogs across the decking.

Watching her walk away, I wait until she is out of earshot before turning to face the others. 'I think someone might finally be feeling a little broody...'

Owen scoffs and shakes his head. 'I don't think so.'

'I *do* think so!' Gina teases, crossing her legs in Marc's lap. 'You should have seen her with the kids at the beach today.'

'She'll get bored, she always does.'

Oliver raises his eyebrows and reaches for his bottle of beer. 'It'll happen for you two. You won't believe it until it does, but it will.'

I nod in agreement and rest my feet on the picnic table. 'And it will be the best thing that ever happened to you.'

'I don't know about that...' He laughs heartily and shakes his head. 'My Maserati is the best thing that ever happened to me.'

A chorus of boos echo around the veranda as Owen chuckles to himself and winks.

'Don't let Eve hear you say that.' Marc teases, pushing his glasses up the bridge of his sunburnt nose.

'Don't let Eve hear you say what?' Squeezing her way through the chairs, Eve places a fresh jug of punch onto the table and flashes Owen an accusing look.

The group falls silent for a moment and I try to rack my brains to think of something to get Owen off the hook.

'We were just saying... we were just saying...' Gina attempts to cover for him, but Owen speaks up.

'This lot are teasing me about you being broody.' Taking a swig of his beer, he taps his knee and motions for her to sit down. 'Can you please tell them that you're not so that we can put a stop to this nonsense?'

Looking out at the ocean, Eve's cheeks turn red as she shrugs her shoulders. 'I guess a baby wouldn't be so bad...'

Gina lets out a whoop as Marc heckles Owen. 'I knew it!' He yells, slapping Owen on the leg. 'I told you!'

'You can't be serious?' Running a hand through his greying hair, he lets out a sigh as Eve nods her head and reaches for her glass.

Suppressing a smile, I take a sip of my punch and rest my head on Oliver's shoulder. Coming from a woman who has stated many times before that she never wants children, this is obviously a huge turnaround, but I always knew that this day would come. With Owen being a good way into his fifties, most of our friends had presumed that they would never have children, but deep down I had a feeling that Eve's biological clock would kick in sooner or later.

'So, what are you saying?' Owen presses, unbuttoning the top button of his shirt.

'I'm saying that I think it is something that we should seriously talk about when we get back home.' Pursing her lips, Eve spins her wedding band around her finger and smiles.

'Good Lord.' Owen laughs and kisses her cheek fondly.

'We all know what that means!' Oliver chuckles, as the rest of the group burst into a fit of giggles.

Joining in with the laughter, I bite my lip and smile to myself. We *do* all know what it means. I don't think there has been a single time in the history of Eve's life that she has wanted something and hasn't gotten it.

'You guys would make great parents.' Gina gushes, not being able to resist giving her two pence worth.

'We most certainly would.' Eve confirms, tucking her blonde hair behind her ear.

'Don't get too ahead of yourself.' Turning a funny shade of purple, Owen finishes his drink and exhales loudly.

'Come on, Owen. We would make *incredible* parents.' Eve smacks her lips together and smiles. 'Just think of what we could give to a child.' Owen's face turns serious for a moment as she stares at him intently. 'We have an amazing home, a good support network and more money than we know what to do with.'

Nodding solemnly, Owen shrugs his shoulders. 'I can't argue with that.'

Knowing that she has won the argument, Eve smothers him in kisses before returning to her hosting. Holding out my glass for a refill, I squeeze her hand briefly before she moves on to Gina. Beneath Owen's reserved exterior, I know that he would take to fatherhood like a duck to water. It's safe to say that Owen is one of the most generous, gentle giants that I have ever met. I have absolutely no doubt in my mind that he will make a fabulous father.

'You could take one of ours for a week.' Gina squeals, sitting bolt upright. 'How about Madison? Or MJ? MJ is probably the best option to ease you into it.'

Looking frankly terrified, Owen lets out a low laugh and excuses himself to go to the bathroom.

'What about Melrose?' She yells after him. 'You can take her for a day or so?' Not waiting for a response, she puts down her drink and chases after him into the house.

'Now look what you have done!' Oliver pokes me in the ribs and laughs.

'Me?' I exclaim, not wanting to take the blame for Gina's hysterics. 'Why is this my fault?'

'Because *you* brought up the whole broody thing!'

Feeling like a naughty schoolgirl who has been scolded by their headmaster, I stick out my tongue and run my fingers through my tangled mane.

'What about you two, anyway?' Stretching out on her lounger, Eve winks and waggles the baby monitor. 'Will there be baby number two any time soon?'

Feeling a little flummoxed, I look at Oliver for help. Believe it or not, more children aren't something that we have discussed before. I mean, I always assumed that we *would* have more children, but now that we have Noah, I just couldn't imagine having enough love to give another child.

'I think we could handle a few more.' Oliver says confidently, peeling the label off his bottle of beer.

Shooting him a startled look, I shake my head and sit up straight. 'Can you please clarify what you mean by *a few?*'

'A few...' He repeats cockily, not missing a beat.

'How many is a few, exactly?' My heart pounds in my chest as I try to work out if he is being serious.

'I dunno. Three... four... five?'

'Five?' I screech, suddenly feeling a little lightheaded. 'Five children?'

Marc lets out a snigger and leans back in his seat, clearly enjoying my pain.

'Why not?' Shrugging his shoulders casually, he reaches over and pulls me towards him.

My cheeks flush pink and I bat his hands away furiously. 'Because for starters it is *me* that will have to give birth to this football team that you plan on having! Not to mention the fact that we are rushed off our feet with Noah.' My mind goes into overdrive as I imagine what our lives would be like if we tossed another five children into the mix. 'We would have to hire help. I would need a nanny, a cleaner... we would have to sell the apartment!'

'Honey, calm down. It was just a joke.' Ruffling my hair, he clinks his bottle against Marc's as they erupt into laughter.

Not seeing the funny side, I push myself to my feet and flounce off across the veranda. Closing the patio doors behind me, I throw myself onto the sofa and strategically place myself beneath the air-conditioning. Joking aside, the thought of more children genuinely petrifies me. I know that Marc and Gina have three, so technically they're more than halfway there, but I am pretty confident that Noah is enough for me. For now, anyway.

Hearing footsteps heading towards me, I peel open an eye to see Gina curling up on the couch opposite.

'Owen's gone to bed.' She grumbles, kicking off her sandals. 'I don't think he is feeling too good.'

'Either that or you have terrified him with the offer of Madison.' Letting out a giggle, I roll onto my side to face her. 'Let's face it, Madison would have Owen wrapped right around her little finger.'

'Madison has *everyone* wrapped around her little finger.' Adjusting her pink hot pants, she motions over to Owen's room and laughs. 'I do think they would make fabulous parents though. I wonder who will have one first, Owen and Eve or Lianna and Vernon?'

'Oh, God!' Clutching my hands to my face, I try to picture Lianna as a mother. As bizarre as it seems right now, I remind myself that I couldn't picture her as a businesswoman either, but she has made Periwinkle into something even Richard Branson would be proud of.

'Can you believe that Lianna is actually doing this?' Gina mumbles.

'After almost ten years of being her best friend, I could believe *anything* of Lianna.' Rolling my eyes, I look up at the ceiling and sigh.

'Very true!' She laughs and starts to reel off all of the ridiculous things that we have known Lianna to do over the years.

From skinny dipping in Ibiza to breaking down in tears over a spilt kebab at the end of a messy night on the tiles, it seems that Lianna has really come a long way.

'I think this is exactly what Lianna needs.' Gina says decidedly.

'You think?'

'I really do. She has to settle down sooner or later and where better to do it than here on Barbados?'

My stomach flips again at the thought of this being Lianna's home. 'You don't think she would really move out here, do you? I just don't think she has it in her to uproot her entire life like that.'

Gina nods and points to the koala tattoo on her ankle. 'Nobody thought *we* would move, but we did.'

'You also came back…' Wagging my finger at her, I feel a lump in my throat as I recall Marc and Gina leaving for the land down under.

I still remember it today. The sinking feeling made me feel physically sick as I stood at the airport with Oliver and Lianna, watching the Strokers disappear up the escalator. To be fair, they did only last a year before they decided that they were going to return to England. Maybe Li will do the same.

'I never believed in soul mates before.' Gina whispers, resting her head in her hands. 'But seeing

the two of them together, it really makes you think.'
Nodding in agreement, I smile as her eyes glaze over.
'It's amazing that two people who have spent just a week together can be so certain that they're meant to be as one. It's pretty special.'

'It is.' I smile, not being able to argue with the very valid points that she has just made.

'Like a modern-day fairy tale...' I mumble, staring up at the ceiling.

'Just like me and Marc...'

Before I can stop it from happening, a snort escapes my lips.

'You can laugh, but I always call Marc my prince.'

'So, does that mean that you think of yourself a princess?' Trying to keep my face natural, I bite the inside of my cheek and smile.

'Now that you say it, a few people have said that I have a look of Snow White.'

She says it so seriously that I almost feel bad for laughing.

'What?' She demands, shooting me daggers.

'Nothing!' I hold up my hands as my stomach throbs with laughter. 'I don't doubt that people think you're a princess. I just wouldn't have put you down as a Snow White that's all...'

'Really?' Gina's eyes sparkle as she starts to reel off different Disney heroines. 'Pocahontas? Jasmine? Belle?'

'Actually, I was thinking more Princess Fiona...'

Chapter 15

Laughing as Madison jumps up and down to the music, I accept another drink from the waitress and watch Stephanie as she dashes around The Hangout. For the past hour, she has whizzed from table to table, refreshing drinks, clearing plates and chatting to the locals. Flashing her a smile as she catches my eye, she nods in response and continues on her way. Putting her dismissiveness down to the fact that she is rushed off her feet, I twist my plastic cup into the sand and take hold of Noah's pram.

Ahead of the stag party tomorrow, Vernon has invited us to The Hangout to meet his friends and family and Lianna has been a skittish mess all morning. Weaving my way through the tables, I prop Noah's pram next to the bar and hop onto a stool. Frantically polishing glasses, it takes her a couple of minutes to realise that I am sitting right in front of her.

'Do you need any help?' I ask, frowning as she knocks over a row of glasses causing them to shatter on the floor.

Bending down to help her clear away the sharp mess, I pull her behind the bar out of the earshot of customers.

'Li, you need to calm down!' Taking her hand in mine, I tuck her hair behind her ear. 'Why are you so worked up?'

Running her fingers beneath her eyes, she lets out a small sob before quickly composing herself. 'I just really want his family to like me.'

'They will like you! What makes you think they wouldn't like you?'

'You!'

'Me?'

'Yes, you!'

'What have I done?'

Curling up next to the champagne fridge, she holds her head in her hands. 'Come on, Clara. As soon as we got engaged you were like - *What are you doing? This is insane! You can't marry someone you have spent just seven days with!*' Looking down at her engagement ring as it sparkles under the bright lights, her bottom lip starts to wobble. 'What if his family say the same thing to him? He might change his mind...'

Chewing the inside of my cheek, I am about to apologise for imposing my perhaps uneducated views onto her when a pair of feet come to an abrupt stop in front of us. Discovering that the feet belong to Stephanie, I fix my face into a smile and pull myself to my feet.

'What happened here?' Her eyes narrow as she takes in the mess on the floor. Exhaling loudly, clearly extremely annoyed, she places the plates in her hand onto the bar and motions for us to leave. 'I'll get it. Vernon is out front. He has been asking for you.'

Scrambling to her feet, Lianna makes an attempt to pull herself together.

'Go to the bathroom and freshen up first.' Grabbing my handbag from Noah's pram, I take my cosmetic bag and shove it into her hands. 'There's some blush and concealer in there.'

Taking the bag, she nods gratefully and slips into the toilets, leaving me alone at the bar. I am lost in thought when Stephanie coughs loudly and I realise that I'm in her way.

'Oops! Sorry!' I attempt a friendly laugh, but she simply shakes her head and gets to work at clearing away the aftermath of a Lianna meltdown.

Oh, dear. It seems that sunny Stephanie has well and truly left the building. Spotting Oliver and the gang monkeying around in the hammocks, I pluck Noah from his pram and make my way across the sand. Their laughter echoes along the beach as they double over in hysterics. Watching Gina unsuccessfully try to climb into a hammock it's easy to see why. Handing Noah to a giggling Oliver, I slip away in search of Vernon.

Luckily, it doesn't take me long to find him. Sitting on a rock at the edge of the water, I couldn't have picked a better time to talk to him if I tried. Slipping off my sunglasses, I take a look around to make sure that we are alone before tapping him on the shoulder.

'Hey.' Taking a seat on an adjacent rock, I kick off my sandals and allow the water to wash over my feet.

'How's it going?' He asks, flipping his phone closed and popping it into his pocket.

'Good.' I mumble, fiddling with my wedding ring. Not wanting to lose my nerve, I take a deep breath before speaking. 'I just wanted to let you know that you have my blessing... with Lianna. I want you to know that I support it one hundred percent. Well, ninety-nine percent at least.'

Hanging his head, he lets out a low laugh and slides onto the rock next to me. 'And what is that final one percent?'

Glancing back up at The Hangout, I spot Lianna with Oliver and smile. 'Being her best friend, I wouldn't be doing my job if I didn't have any concerns about her marrying a man who she has known for such a short period of time.' He nods in agreement and stares solemnly back at me. 'A man who lives on a Caribbean island, four thousand miles away from home. A man who I spent approximately five days with before he decided that he was going to marry her.'

Not taking his eyes off mine, Vernon reaches over and takes my hand in his.

'I'm going to be completely honest with you. I have the exact same concerns that you have.'

My stomach drops through the floor as his words hit me.

'Don't you think I have had this exact conversation with my own friends and family? Every time somebody looks at me the way you are doing right now, I question myself. I mean, what the hell am I doing here? Am I crazy? Have I totally lost touch with reality?' Laughing gently, he shakes his head and looks out to sea. 'Of all of the beautiful women I see every day, I had to go and fall in love with a British chick. But you know what? Lianna is the best thing that has ever happened to me.' His brown eyes sparkle as a huge smile spreads across his face. 'I knew the moment that I laid eyes on her that she was the woman I would marry. I just never dreamed that she would feel the same way that I did.'

Pursing my lips, I suddenly feel a little sorry for him. He's just a guy who met a girl and fell in love. Since when was that a crime? Let's face it, when you find that real, inconvenient, all-consuming, once in a lifetime kind of love, you don't care about timings and logistics.

'I know that what we are doing isn't strictly conventional and I can't promise you that I know what happens next, because I don't. But I *can* promise you that I will make it my mission in life to make Li happy. Whatever it takes and wherever it takes me...' A lump forms in the back of my throat as he squeezes my arm encouragingly. 'I understand that nothing I say will stop you from worrying completely, but it means a lot to both of us that we have your blessing.'

Not wanting to speak in case I burst into tears, I resort to a swift nod of the head as I attempt to regain the use of my tongue. I am about to throw my arms around his neck when a clatter of commotion causes him to jump to his feet. Spinning around, I see a crowd of people heading across the sand towards us. Waving their arms around merrily, I have no doubt in my mind that these are Vernon's family. As Vernon excuses himself and runs over to a plump elderly lady, I discreetly slip away and make my way back to Oliver and the gang.

MJ is the first to spot me and dives between the palm trees before throwing himself into my arms. Tipping him upside down, I tickle his stomach as I collapse into a chair.

'Did you give him *the talk*?' Marc asks, taking MJ and sitting him in a hammock.

Shooting him a puzzled look, I feel Lianna's eyes burning into the back of my head.

'You know!' Marc presses, his eyes glinting mischievously. 'The – *hurt my best friend and I will hunt you down and kill you* talk?'

'You didn't? Lianna gasps, slapping my arm. 'Clara!'

Holding my hands up in defence, I shake my head. 'I didn't have to. He beat me to it.'

Lianna squints her eyes suspiciously and crosses her arms, clearly very annoyed.

'Honestly.' I attempt a smile, but she doesn't return it. 'He's a good guy, Li. You're lucky to have him.'

The rest of the group nods in agreement as Eve smiles smugly. 'I'm not going to say I told you so, but I told you so!'

Rolling my eyes, I twist my hair up and secure it beneath my cap. Laughter travels up the beach as Lianna lets out a whimper.

'Oh, God! Is this his family?' Her pupils dilate as she takes in the group of people walking towards us.

The rest of the group strain their necks for a better look. They seem a happy bunch, that's for sure. The palm trees rustle in the sea breeze, drowning out the majority of their conversation as they walk towards us. Feeling Lianna's sweaty hand squeeze my shoulder, I shoot her a reassuring smile. Bless her. She looks genuinely terrified. Not having the time to give her a pep talk, I resort to a quick squeeze of the hand.

Popping his sunglasses onto his head, Vernon slings an arm around the shoulder of a tiny lady with a headful of beautiful curls.

'Guys, this is my mom, Cora.'

A chorus of hello echoes around the group as we jump to our feet. Grabbing Noah from Oliver before he can throw a tantrum, I stand to the side and push Lianna forward.

Not saying a word, Li twirls a strand of sun-bleached hair around her finger and smiles nervously.

Obviously sensing how anxious she is, Vernon holds out his hand for hers. Not missing a beat, Cora's eyes land on Lianna's sapphire clad finger.

'Hi, Mrs Clarke.' Lianna mumbles, looking more frightened than ever.

Her voice is tiny as the rest of us hold our breath. Taking a tiny step forward, Cora's face breaks into a huge smile as she throws her arms around Lianna and plants a big red kiss on her cheek. Locking eyes with Oliver, he flashes me a wink as the rest of us breathe a sigh of relief.

Taking Lianna's face in her hands, Cora lets out an elated laugh and squeals. 'Welcome to the family, my darling.'

* * *

Two hours later, it is safe to say that Lianna has been welcomed into the Clarke family with open arms. Cora Clarke, who I have to admit is quite possibly the nicest person I have ever met in my entire life, seems even more in love with Lianna than Vernon himself. From invites to Florida to meet extended members of the family, to the offer of Cora's earrings for her something old, Lianna couldn't have asked for a more positive first meeting. And it's not only Cora who has taken a shine to Li. Daniel, Vernon's younger brother, has given her his seal of approval, too. Not to mention Vernon's golfing buddies, who just can't seem to get enough of Lianna's amazing British accent. Unfortunately, my own British accent doesn't seem to have the same magic as Lianna's.

Picking up a handful of sand and letting it fall between my fingers, I glance into Noah's pram to check that he is still asleep. With the rest of the group chatting merrily, I have decided to take a back seat and observe the festivities. To be honest, I am completely wiped and watching Noah snooze is making me want to do the exact same thing.

The sun is now low in the sky, casting a cosy shadow across the beach and encasing us in a safe bubble. Tipping back my head, I flash Oliver a smile as Eve crashes down beside me.

'I'm going for another.' Waving her empty glass around happily, she hiccups and clasps a hand to her mouth. 'Want one?'

'No.' I laugh and take the glass from her. 'I don't think you should be having another either.'

Frowning like a naughty toddler, she pokes her head into Noah's pram and sighs. 'I want one of those.'

'What?' I ask, giggling at her intoxicated state. 'A nap?'

Shaking her head wildly, she hiccups again and laughs. 'No! Not a nap, a baby.'

'Well, right now I think you have got more chance of a nap.' Ruffling her hair, I lock eyes with Owen and beckon him over.

'I think someone needs to go home.' Tilting my head towards Eve, I roll my eyes as Owen finishes his drink and pulls Eve to her feet.

'No!' Eve mumbles, attempting to take off her sandals. 'The party is just getting started!'

'Not for you it isn't.' He laughs and plants a kiss on her forehead. 'I'll call a car.' Digging his phone out of his pocket, he jabs at the keys and does a quick headcount. 'Are you guys ready to head back, too?'

Nodding in agreement, I reach for my flip-flops and wave my arms around to get Oliver's attention. Totally engrossed in conversation with Daniel, he doesn't seem to notice the crazy octopus lady behind him. Leaving Noah with Owen, I squeeze through the hammocks and slip my arm around Oliver's waist.

'Eve has had a little too much to drink, so we are going to head back to the villa. Do you want to stay here for a while or are you ready to come back with us?'

'You guys aren't going already, are you?' Daniel yells, throwing an arm around my neck. 'We're meant to be celebrating!'

Looking down at his empty bottle of beer, Oliver screws up his nose, obviously torn.

'I don't mind.' I offer him a smile and look over my shoulder at Eve. 'Honestly, you stay and enjoy yourself.'

'What a woman!' Laughing loudly, Daniel shouts to Vernon to get more beer.

'Actually, I think I am gonna go back. Save myself for tomorrow.'

'What's happening tomorrow?' I ask, accepting a kiss goodbye from Daniel.

'You're joking, right?' Daniel's eyes widen and I can't help but laugh. 'It's the bachelor party!'

'Oh...' I nod as I remember the all-important event. 'In that case, you're *definitely* coming back now. Let's go.'

Leaving Oliver to say his goodbyes, I round up Marc and Gina before dragging Lianna away from her adoring public.

'Aren't they incredible?' She gushes, bobbing her head as music drifts out of The Hangout. 'I couldn't have wished for better, I really, really couldn't.' A smile spreads across my face as she beams from ear to ear. 'I'm so happy, Clara.'

Pulling her in for a hug, I plant a kiss on her cheek and squeeze her tightly. 'I know you are and I'm truly happy for you.' Tearing myself away, I point over to where Eve is swaying. 'We have got to get Eve to bed, so we're going to go now, but you have a fabulous evening and I shall see you tomorrow. What time are you coming over?'

'I think Vernon has arranged to collect the guys at seven...' She screws her nose up uncertainly and bites her finger. 'Or was it eight... I can't remember which.'

'Eight? Isn't that a little late for fishing?'

'Yeah... I think the whole fishing thing went out of the window when Daniel arrived.'

Glancing over at Vernon who is goofing around with his golfing buddies, I dread to think what they have planned for him. Not wanting to think about it, I shake my head and laugh.

'Either way, I will see you tomorrow.' Blowing her a kiss, I slide my sunglasses up into my hair and smile. 'Text me.'

Owen catches my eye and points to Noah who is now screaming in his pram. Quickly saying my goodbyes to Cora and Vernon, I wrench Oliver away from Daniel as the Strokers start to make their way along the beach to the waiting car.

Handing Noah to Oliver, I collapse the pram and follow the sound of Eve's drunken ramblings. Madison throws her sandals into the sand and refuses to walk, resulting in Marc throwing her over his shoulder like a fireman. Looking back at Lianna laughing heartily with Vernon and his family, a lump forms in the back of my throat. My mother once told me that happiness does not depend on what you have; it relies solely on how you think. Seeing Li so overjoyed at the prospect of a last-minute wedding without a care in the world as to what she wears, where she does it or who is there to witness it, I can't help but think that no truer words were ever spoken...

Chapter 16

Snapping photographs of Noah as he splashes around in the pool with Oliver, I feel my heart pang with love. Today has probably been my favourite day since we arrived on the island over a week ago. The weather has been kind enough to cool down a few degrees and we even had a spot of rain earlier. Now, you might find it strange that a British person who flees the UK every six months in a desperate bid for some Vitamin D would be happy about having grey skies whilst on holiday. However, after seven days of intense Caribbean heat, the feeling of cool raindrops splashing down onto my skin was greatly appreciated.

Tossing my camera into the beach bag, I slide into the water. It is almost criminal that we haven't used this incredible pool until now. With breathtaking views of the azure blue ocean ahead, Eve's stunning infinity pool is almost as beautiful as the ocean itself. The intricate mosaic tiles glisten beneath the water as the sun peeks through the clouds. Swimming over to Oliver, I pull Noah in his baby floater and laugh as he squeals when the water splashes his face. With Vernon not due to arrive for the stag-do until later, we decided to make the most of the day and abuse Eve's frankly fabulous facilities.

'I can't wait to see Lianna's dress!' Spinning around to face Oliver, I slip my shoulders beneath the surface of the water. 'They should be back any minute now.'

'I thought you had already seen it?' He mumbles, shaking water out of his eyes.

'I have, but not since Delores has altered it.' Holding Noah's hands as he kicks his legs frantically, I stick my tongue out at him as he squeals. 'She looked incredible, Oliver. Vernon will be blown away.'

'They're back!' Madison yells, poking her head out of the patio doors.

Suppressing a scream, I am about to make for the steps when Lianna and Eve run out onto the veranda.

'How did it go?' I ask, shielding my eyes from the sun. 'In fact, don't tell me. Let me get dry and you can show me!'

'You're wasting your breath.' Eve sighs, rolling up her dress and dipping her feet into the water.

'What's going on?' Shooting her a quizzical look, I rest my elbows on the edge of the pool.

Lianna opens her mouth to speak, but Eve beats her to it.

'She won't try the damn thing on! Delores kindly gave her a veil as a gift, but she won't try that on either.'

'What?' Turning to face Lianna, I adjust my swimming costume and walk out of the water. 'Why?'

'Because I don't want to decide that I don't like it, that's why.' Turning on her heels, she throws the dress bag over her shoulder and disappears inside.

'But but what if it doesn't fit?' Grabbing a towel from the sun lounger, I wrap it around myself and chase after her. 'You *have* to try it on!'

'Nope. I'm not putting it on until the day.' Obviously not wanting to back down, she carefully places the bag into her rental car and swaps it for a rucksack before beeping the key fob.

I look at Gina for help, but she simply shrugs her shoulders indicating that she doesn't want to get involved. Taking a bikini out of the rucksack, she shakes off her Birkenstock sandals and disappears into the bathroom to change.

Leaning against the door, I pat myself down and throw the towel onto the dining room table. 'Li, if you don't try it on and it doesn't fit on the day, what are you going to do?'

'It *will* fit.' She fires back confidently. 'If I remember correctly, you never tried your wedding dress on before the big day.'

'That was because I didn't *choose* my dress, you know that.'

Bugger. I should have known that she would use that against me. For those of you who don't know, Oliver secretly planned our wedding from start to finish. I actually didn't even know that I was getting married at all until an hour before the event itself. Not conventional, I know, but I wouldn't have it any other way.

Throwing open the bathroom door, she flashes me a smile and scrunches up her dress. 'It will be *fine*. Now come on, let's get in the pool.'

Holding my hands up to surrender, I grab Madison as she makes a beeline for the doors. 'Not so fast, lady.' Handing her over to Gina to be smothered in sun lotion, I steal a crisp from Marc before wandering back outside into the sunshine.

Jumping back into the water, I pull Noah into the shade as the pool starts to fill up with people. First Lianna, then Eve, and before long, everyone but Owen is splashing around in the water.

'So, are you boys looking forward to the stag-do tonight?' Eve asks, letting MJ climb onto her shoulders.

'Yes, ma'am.' Oliver laughs, looking at Marc and winking.

'I saw that.' Wagging her finger at Oliver, Gina splashes water on Marc and slips Melrose into a baby floater. 'Don't forget, after you've had *your* fun tonight, it's *our* turn tomorrow! Isn't that right, ladies?'

Lianna and Eve let out whoops as Oliver shakes his head. 'Don't you think it's a little dangerous to have a bachelorette party the night before a wedding?'

'We could always swap the days around? Li offers, winking at Gina. 'We could take on whatever you have planned for tonight and you can have our relaxing spa day...'

'I think we're good.' Raising his eyebrows, Oliver lets Madison dunk him under the water playfully.

'You're very calm.' Marc observes, paddling over to Lianna. 'You do know that you're getting married in forty-eight hours, don't you?'

'Really? I did *not* know that.' Rolling her eyes, she holds up her giant rock and waggles it in his face.

Splashing her with water, he attempts to get away before she can get her revenge. Not letting him get away with wetting her hair, she dives under the water and attempts to pull him under. As the entire pool turns into a free for all, I take Noah and scramble to the safety of the sun loungers, laughing as Gina lets out a squeal and follows suit. Watching them laugh and shout as they goof around in the sunshine, I plant a kiss on Noah's head and smile. It's moments like this that prove laughter is timeless, imagination has no age and dreams last forever...

* * *

'How do you think the boys are getting on?' Clinking my glass against Lianna's, I shove a handful of pretzels into my mouth.

When Vernon rolled up in a ridiculous black limousine earlier, Marc, Owen and Oliver looked like all their Christmases had come at once. The packed-out limo was filled to the brim with champagne, beer and more rum than I ever thought possible. Even James managed to bag an invite to the exclusive party. With promises to be on their best behaviour we waved them off into the sunset.

'I think at least one of them has thrown up.' Gina laughs and reaches for the pretzels. 'Probably Marc.'

'Eww!' Eve screws her nose up and turns the music up a little.

With the children safely snoozing in the bedrooms, we decided to take it easy tonight and spend the night eating takeout pizza. In hindsight, pizza probably wasn't the best idea given that Lianna is getting married in a couple of days. Looking at her now with a swollen stomach and barbecue sauce on her chin, I suppress a giggle and collapse into a heap beside her.

'You look a mess.' I laugh and hand her a napkin. 'It's a good job that Vernon can't see you right now. He might change his mind.'

Slapping my arm, she tries and fails to remove the offending sauce from her chin. 'I think you will find that Vernon loves me for the person that I am on the *inside*. He doesn't care about what I look like on the *outside*.'

'You sure about that?' Gina scoffs, waving her wine glass around erratically. 'Just wait until you've had three kids and things start going south...'

'Just ignore her.' Eve tuts and confiscates Gina's glass.

'That's easy for you to say.' Retrieving her lip gloss from her pocket, Gina makes a poor attempt at topping up her lip colour. 'Even I fancy you.'

Eve's cheeks blush pink as she brushes off the compliments. 'Don't be ridiculous.'

Breathing in my muffin top, I roll off the couch and grab a bottle of water from the fridge. A warm breeze drifts in through the open patio doors, enticing me out onto the veranda.

'I'm going outside for some air.' Lianna announces, as though reading my mind.

Fastening the cap on the bottle of water, I follow her through the living room.

'I'll get more drinks.' Gina yells, making her way into the kitchen and nearly falling several times in the process.

Clearly not wanting to let Gina loose in her prized drinks cabinet, Eve dashes after her and hides a bottle of luxury rum under the sink. Swallowing the laugh that is growing in my stomach, I abandon my sandals and slip outside. Scanning the veranda, it takes me a moment to realise that the white rock down at the water's edge is actually Lianna. The warm air smothers me as I wander across the soft sand, making me want to curl up right here on the beach.

Dropping down next to her, I stick my toes into the water and I'm surprised to discover that it is still rather warm. Lianna shakes her hair back in the breeze and frowns when she realises that I haven't brought any drinks.

'I think we should save ourselves until tomorrow, don't you?' Tucking her hair behind her ears, I can't help but notice that she is rather intoxicated.

Letting out a little snort, she drops her head onto my shoulder and sighs. 'I'm getting married.'

'Yes, Lianna. Yes, you are.' I look out at the shimmering ocean and think about just how much has happened on this holiday. 'You aren't having second thoughts, are you?'

Shaking her head furiously, she stretches out her legs on the sand. 'Nope. You know, you have asked me that same question a thousand times, are you hoping that I will change my mind?'

'Not at all.' Looking down at my knees, I dust the sand off my shins and sigh. 'I just want you to know that you don't *have* to do anything that you aren't one hundred percent comfortable with.'

Li rubs her nose and succeeds only in getting sand all over her face. 'I want to tell you something, but I don't want you to get upset...'

Her words trail off as she looks away guiltily. What the hell has she done now?

'What the hell have you done now?' My mind races with all the dreadful, or rather stupid things that Lianna has done over the years and a bead of sweat crawls down my forehead as I wait for her to spill the beans. 'Spit it out!' I yell, not being able to stand the anticipation for a second longer.

Rubbing her eyes, she stays silent for what seems like forever before finally relenting. 'It's Stephanie.'

I screw up my nose in confusion. 'What about Stephanie?'

'It was her.'

'What was?'

'Everything!' Li throws her hands in the air angrily. 'Everything that went wrong at The Hangout, it was all her.'

Twisting my hair out of my face, I try to process what she is saying, or rather *trying* to say in her drunken state.

'The kitchen errors, the guest list incident, the prawn hidden in the fish curry...' Her voice trails off into inaudible mumbles as she shakes her head furiously.

'Fish curry?' I look at her as though she has lost her mind and wonder if I should fetch a sick bucket.

'She was intentionally trying to sabotage things, Clara! That's why she took the job in the first place. She was only there to ruin The Hangout!'

'No way!' As I gaze back at her, the words finally sink in. 'Bloody hell! She came across so well, too. That's crazy.' Staring out at the ocean, I remind myself that she *was* poached from a rival bar, some people would say that if you play with fire, you're probably going to get burned.

'Vern fired her...' She mumbles, her voice suddenly small.

'Well, I guessed that.' Secretly feeling a little relieved that her big revelation isn't something more catastrophic, I wiggle my toes in the sand and exhale slowly.

We sit in a comfortable silence for a moment, both of us drawing patterns into the damp sand.

'I'm going to take her job.' She suddenly announces, causing me to burst into laughter.

Hiccupping loudly, she nods vigorously to show how serious she is. 'I know you think it's the rum talking, but it isn't.'

'OK...' She has clearly had more to drink than I first thought. 'Let's talk about this tomorrow, shall we?'

Not wanting to get into a drunken rambling with a tipsy Li, I decide to ignore her and attempt to change the subject.

'Are you looking forward to...'

'I'm not *that* drunk, Clara.' Furrowing her brow, she reaches over and takes my hand. '*I am* going to stay out here.'

'You *can't* just stay out here. It doesn't work like that.' Pursing her lips defiantly, she twirls her ring around her finger, an unreadable expression on her face. 'Even if you're married, you still need to apply for a visa. Plus, you've got a thriving business back in London. Not to mention a house, a car...' My words drift off into babbles as my heart rate picks up. 'You can't just *stay!*'

Laughing loudly, Lianna throws herself back onto the sand rolls onto her stomach. 'I know that, but I *am* going to live here. You know, when I have sorted out the legalities.'

'But... but... but what are you going to do about Periwinkle? You have put years into building it up. You can't just walk away from it.'

'Of course, I'm not going to walk away from it!' She looks up at me as if I am stupid and rolls her eyes. 'I'm going to sell it.'

'*Sell* it!' I squeal, feeling like my heart is going to pound out of my chest. 'Lianna! You can't!'

'I can and I shall. I am going to use the money to buy into The Hangout. That way I will still have a business and an income, so you can stop worrying!' Pulling my arm so that I tumble down beside her, she rests her head on my shoulder. 'You don't need to babysit me anymore. I appreciate you looking out for me, I really, really do, but I am a big girl now.'

Not taking my eyes off hers, I exhale slowly and shake my head. I have lost count of the number of times that Lianna and I have had this same conversation in the past. Each and every time Li has one of her crazy, spontaneous ideas, we have the same heart to heart that always ends in the same way. I tell her that she is far too impulsive and makes life-changing decisions without putting any thought into it and she tells me that I have to stop mothering her and let her live her own life. In the end, I give in, she makes a decision that I don't agree with and when it all inevitably falls apart, I pick up the pieces.

'This isn't like all those stupid decisions that I have made in the past. I *know* what I am doing this time.' I let out a laugh and tear my eyes away. So, this is what deja-vu feels like. 'Don't you think I want what you and Marc both have? Don't you think a part of me hates seeing my two best friends *so* happy when I know that I haven't even come close to finding happiness myself?'

'Lianna...'

'When you met Oliver, you didn't know how important he was going to become to you. If I would have told you back then, seven days after meeting him that he was going to be your husband, the father of your child and your one true love, you would probably run as fast as you could in the other direction.' Not being able to argue with her, I rub my temples as she continues. 'That is why I am so confident that this is right for me. What did I say to you when I returned from Barbados last year?'

A smile plays on the corner of my lips as I recall picking her up from the airport. Her skin was golden, her eyes sparkling as she dived into the passenger seat of my car. Before I could even say *hi,* she burst into a fit of giggles and clasped her hands over her heart.

'You said that you had met the man that you were going to spend the rest of your life with.'

'And that, Clara is *exactly* what I am going to do...'

Chapter 17

'To Lianna.' Eve takes her glass of bubbles and holds it high in the air. 'I wish you and Vernon a lifetime of happiness together.'

'To Lianna.' Gina and I raise our glasses and clink them against Eve's as Li's cheeks turn pink.

Smiling as I take a sip of the ice-cold bubbles, I pull my robe tightly around my body and look down at my glossy nails. For the past couple of hours, the four of us have been holed up at a luxury spa on the west coast. After a rather fabulous top to toe massage, we have been treated to a relaxing pedicure and my once unloved toenails are now sparkling like crazy under the bright lights of the salon. Looking over at Lianna who hasn't stopped smiling all day, I can't deny that this hen-do has gotten off to a superb start.

When we left the villa this morning, the boys were more than a little worse for wear. It would seem that a night out drinking rum and God knows what else until the early hours of the morning results in one hell of a hangover. Eve and I spent an hour quizzing Owen and Oliver, trying to get the gory details out of them. Despite our mammoth efforts, all we got were that Marc threw up, Owen lost a load of money in a game of dominoes and Oliver fell asleep on the way home. I think it's safe to say that Lianna's party won't be anywhere *near* as crazy.

Taking a sip of bubbles, I thank the lovely ladies who have been beautifying us and stretch out on the padded lounger. This time tomorrow, Li will be getting ready to walk down the aisle. Well, down the sand. After our drunken conversation last night, I woke up more than a little concerned about my best friend, but looking at her now I couldn't be happier for her if I tried.

'How do you feel?' Eve asks, placing her glass down on the wooden table in front of her.

Exhaling loudly, Lianna shakes her head and smiles. 'I don't know! Excited, happy, thrilled, ecstatic...'

'I remember the night before my wedding.' Gina muses, running a hand through her black locks.

'How did you feel?' Lianna looks down at her pretty pink nails and smiles.

'In a word... *drunk!*'

I let out a laugh and down the contents of my glass. I don't think there has a been a time in Gina's life where she *hasn't* felt drunk. Checking my watch, I pull the towelling headband out of my hair and push myself to my feet. If I sit here any longer, I am most definitely going to drift off.

'What's next on the agenda, bride-to-be?' Holding out a hand to pull her up, I slip my mobile phone into my robe pocket.

Lianna scratches her nose and takes out our room key. I say *our* room key because we are all in the same room. Well, to call it a room isn't really fair, the enormous, ocean-front suite is almost as big as Eve's villa. I'm kind of gutted that I only get to spend one night in it.

'Well, we have dinner booked for seven and then I thought we could have cocktails on the balcony?'

Gina and Eve nod in agreement and follow Lianna out of the spa. Tagging along behind, we walk along the corridor until we come to the lift.

With the marriage ceremony due to take place late in the afternoon, us girls are staying here tonight before heading back to the villa to get ready in the morning. Despite our efforts, Li still protests that she will only need an hour to prepare for her nuptials. Not wanting to argue with the future Mrs Clarke, I decided to take a back seat and let her take charge. As far as I am aware, she hasn't let Eve and Gina in on her plans to move to Barbados. After my not so positive reaction, she is probably going to be a little more careful with who she divulges this information to. I must admit that I expected her to wake up this morning and tell me that she didn't mean what she was saying last night, but it was much the opposite. Over our delicious bacon and eggs courtesy of James, Li threw back two pain killers and made it very clear that she was just as determined as she was last night to go through with her plans to sell Periwinkle and flee the UK.

I must admit that I did let Oliver in on her momentous decision and surprisingly, he thought that it was the right thing for Lianna. The way that he sees it, is that Lianna is now a rather wealthy young woman with no responsibilities. With her having a house, a car and a business I beg to differ, but he has opened my eyes to his way of thinking. Apparently, Vernon had opened up to Oliver on his stag-do about Stephanie's shady antics and he is ecstatic that Lianna has decided to sell up and join him here in Barbados.

'It's such a shame that Cora didn't want to join us.' Eve sighs, stepping into the lift and immediately checking out her reflection in the mirror.

'After listening to Gina's stories the other day, I'm not surprised that she decided to give it a miss, are you?' Shaking my head at Gina, I break out in a fit of giggles as I remember Cora's face when Gina revealed all about Lianna's crazy, single girl antics.

The lift doors ping open and we pile out into the corridor. As we wait for Lianna to work out how to use the room card, I wander over to the window and look down at the scene below. Barbados is quite possibly the most beautiful island that I have ever visited. A few beach bums stretch out on the sand, desperate to soak up the last of the afternoon sun. Resting my head against the glass, I watch a flock of birds dance around in the sky before swooping off into the sunset. I can't quite believe that in a few short days I shall be back in England, back in my city centre apartment in lively London.

For a split second a wave of jealously washes over me. This is going to be Lianna's home. Her *home*. The place where she returns to after a long day at the job. I am suddenly reminded that Li's work is going to involve, a beach, rum punch, flying fish burgers and not much else. A pretty big change to darting around London all day with a clipboard and a headset. She's going to be living the dream. Why haven't I seen that before now? Most people would chop their legs off for a chance to make this their reality. Tearing myself away from the window, I throw my arm around Lianna's neck and plant a kiss on her cheek. Suddenly her decision to move out here doesn't seem so ridiculous after all...

* * *

'Today has been... perfect.' Lianna gushes. 'Honestly, really, really perfect.'

Looking out over the still black water, I can't help but agree with her. If I could have my wedding day all over again, this is exactly how I would do it. From the laid-back arrangements to the chilled-out hen-do, I really would copy every single detail. No one has stressed out about the cake, the flowers or the seating plan. No one has had a break down about the missing rings, the uncontactable caterer or the fact that we have had a few drops of rain, it really has been more perfect than perfect could be.

Resisting the urge to call Oliver again to check on the babies, I slip my phone into my handbag and kick it under the table in front of me. After a delicious three-course meal, more glasses of bubbles than I can care to remember and the world's best massage, all I can think about is crawling into the huge bed that is waiting for me inside.

'This time tomorrow, you will be a married woman.' Gina muses, stretching out her legs and almost tippling over in her chair. 'You will be one of us.'

'One of us?' Li asks, frowning as she tips her glass upside down and realises that it's empty.

'A *wife*.' Eve laughs. 'Welcome to the club!'

We clink our now empty glasses together and fall about laughing. The moon shines brightly down upon us as we drop into a comfortable silence. I think we can safely say that we are all completely beat. Resting my head on my shoulder, I take a deep breath and inhale the salty sea air. The noise from the bar below comes to a sudden stop and I am about to suggest that we call it a night when Gina speaks up.

'So, how is this going to work then?' Gina asks, letting out a rather unladylike burp. 'You and Vernon, how is it going to work?'

Bloody hell, Gina. We were so close to getting through the night without any awkward moments. Mentally cursing Gina, I lock eyes with Li and bite my lip. Holding my breath, I chew the inside of my cheek anxiously and look out over the water.

'Well...' She pauses for a moment, as though choosing her words carefully. 'I am going to sell Periwinkle and move out here as soon as possible.'

Gina shoots me an alarmed look as her brow furrows in confusion. Not wanting to upset Lianna, I decide to stay out of it.

'What about your house?' Eve asks, tucking her hair behind her ears. 'And your car?'

'I'm going to sell those, too.'

A few questions arise as to why and how she came to this decision. As Lianna tells the story of Stephanie's shady behaviour once again, I find myself strangely mesmerised. A few gasps escape Gina's lips as she takes in the fact that Stephanie deliberately sabotaged The Hangout. Even now on my second time of hearing it, I still find it hard to believe, but as Eve is quick to point out, hiring from a rival company is not the brightest idea. As Lianna finally stops for breath, I look around the group and prepare myself for the chaos. Surprisingly, it doesn't come.

'I think that's fabulous.' Eve breathes. 'Seriously, I think it is amazing. Well done, Lianna. I think you and Vernon will be extremely happy here in Barbados.'

'I second that.' Rolling onto her side, Gina smiles broadly and touches Li's arm. 'You deserve it.'

Lianna looks around the balcony as her eyes fill up with tears.

'Don't cry!' I let out a little laugh and throw my arms around her neck. 'Those had better be happy tears!'

Nodding as she attempts to wipe her eyes, she erupts into giggles as Gina and Eve throw themselves into the scrum. Trying to compose herself, she bats us away and holds a napkin under her eyes. The sea breeze blows her hair as she pads across the balcony and leans over the railing before turning back to face us.

'I just want to say the biggest thank you possible to all of you. I know that this isn't the most conventional way to do things and I know that none of you would probably even dream of doing things this way.'

'When have you ever done anything the conventional way?' Gina cackles, causing us all to burst into laughter.

Putting down her glass, Lianna lets out a giggle and shakes her head. 'Exactly, but I can't thank you enough for not judging me, for this or for any of the other crazy things that I get myself into.'

Eve and Gina rush over and envelope Li into a huge bear hug. A wave of emotion rises in my throat and before I can stop it from happening, tears spill down my cheeks. Not wanting to speak in case I erupt into a blubbering mess, I resort to raising my empty glass to the sky.

'To Lianna. You smile, I smile. You cry, I cry. Whatever makes you happy, makes me happy.' Gina and Eve scramble around for their glasses and hold them against mine. 'You're my best friend and I love you.' I flash her a wink and swallow the lump in my throat. 'To Lianna.'

'To Lianna...'

Chapter 18

The first thing that hits me when I peel open my eyes is the sun blaring through the huge floor to ceiling windows. The second thing that hits me is the fact that Lianna's ridiculously knobbly knees are wedged into my back. Stretching my arms out above my head, I let out a lion worthy yawn and lift my head up before letting it crash back down onto the plush pillow. My eyes automatically close again and I allow myself a few moments of delicious snoozing before forcing myself to roll over.

Lianna looks so incredibly angelic as she sleeps that I almost don't want to wake her. Curled up into a tiny ball with her long blonde hair sprawled out behind her she could pass for a child. Well, long limbs and belly button piercing aside. I strain my ears and try to work out if the others are awake. Judging by the snoring that it is drifting through the walls, I can safely say that at least *one* of them is still in the land of nod. I'd put my money on Gina.

Kicking off the sheets, I twist my hair into something that can only resemble a bird's nest and pad across the warm tiles. Grabbing my sunglasses from the dressing table, I push open the balcony doors and collapse into a chair. It is still early in the morning, but the sun is already in full bloom. For once, the water is serenely still, as though it knows that something monumental is happening today. It's certainly a beautiful day for a wedding, that's for sure.

I look out at the soft white sand and find myself wondering how many weddings have happened here, how many couples keep this place safe in their heart and how many times the ocean has heard those iconic words, *I do.*

Checking my watch, I am suddenly reminded of just how much we have to do and decide to wake the troops. Making my way back inside, I drop down onto the bed beside Lianna and tap her arm gently.

'Li...' Waiting for her to stir, I give her a minute before resorting to a sharp nudge. 'Li, time to wake up.'

Not getting the response that I wanted, I bounce up and down on the bed before shaking her firmly. 'Lianna!' I whisper, a little louder than I anticipated.

Moving her hair out of her face, I let out a laugh when I realise that she has been drooling into her pillow. Only Lianna could sleep like a bloody baby the night before her own wedding. Most women spend the eve of their wedding tossing and turning, having cold sweats about the millions of things that could possibly go wrong.

I am debating throwing a jug of water on her when she wakes herself up with her own snoring. Letting out a moan, she screws up her nose and tugs the sheets back over her head.

'Lianna!' I yell, jumping onto the bed and dragging the covers away from her. 'It's your *wedding* day! You have to get up!'

Kicking her legs around like an angry toddler, she curls up into a ball and covers her face with her hair. 'Just five more minutes...'

You have got to be kidding me. Throwing open the drapes, I walk across the room and knock on Eve's bedroom door. Not getting a response, I let myself in and wander over to the bed. Surprised to find it empty, I wander around the room and follow the sound of laughter out onto the balcony.

'You're finally up then.' I shield my eyes from the sun and lean on the back of Eve's chair.

'We have been up for hours, *actually*.' Gina sticks her tongue out and stretches out her legs.

'Really?' I ask, creasing my brow into a frown. 'Well, in that case, you had better call down to housekeeping and get them to remove the piglet that I heard snoring before.'

Eve lets out a giggle as Gina reaches behind her chair and smacks my arm playfully.

'Where's the bride-to-be?' Gina asks, looking down at her wrist for her watch and realising it's not there.

'The future Mrs Clarke is still in the land of nod.' Scratching my head, I motion towards the bedroom. 'Despite my numerous attempts to get her up, she begged, or rather *growled*, for five more minutes.'

'Well, she can't have five more minutes!' Eve shrieks. 'She's getting married today!'

'Really? Someone should have mentioned that earlier...' Rolling her eyes, Gina pushes herself to her feet and heads inside. 'I'll get her up.'

'Let's all go.' Eve declares, chasing after Gina and tugging me with her.

Turning on the television as we pass, I manage to flick to the music channels before Eve pulls me into the bedroom. Blissfully unaware that she is being surrounded, Lianna snores away in her pit like a happy puppy.

Upbeat reggae music fills the room as Gina gives Lianna a swift dig in the ribs. 'Come on, Miss Edwards. It's time to get married...'

* * *

'You can't be serious?' Eve gasps, shaking her head in disbelief as Lianna swings into a burger joint and pulls on the handbrake. 'You *can't* have a bloody cheeseburger for breakfast!'

'I can and I will.' Unbuckling her seatbelt, she flashes us a smile and winks before diving out of the car. 'Anyone want anything?'

'It's your *wedding* day!' Eve protests loudly. 'We should be having smoked salmon, croissants and champagne! Looking at Gina and I for backup, she motions for Li to get back into the car.

'I don't want smoked salmon.' Lifting her vest top to scratch her belly, Li screws up her nose and adjusts her shorts. 'Last chance, does anyone want anything?'

'I guess I could eat a burger.' Gina sighs, sliding across the seat and making a grab for her handbag. 'Clara?'

Not daring to look Eve in the eye, I shrug my shoulders and push open the car door. Eve's cheeks turn pink as she realises that she's outnumbered.

'It's her day.' I whisper, jumping onto the pavement. 'Just let her do it her way.'

Finally relenting, Eve lets out a sigh and steps out of the car. A cheeseburger with fries isn't the most traditional wedding breakfast in the world, but it couldn't be more *Lianna* if it tried. Traipsing across the car park, I intentionally keep a few steps behind as my mobile vibrates in my back pocket. Handing Eve my purse, I ask her to grab me anything and flip open the handset.

'Hello?'

'Hey.' Oliver's familiar voice comes down the line bringing an automatic smile to my face. 'Where are you guys at?'

After confirming that we survived the hen night and that we are indeed on our way, I quiz Oliver about how things are holding up at his end. Call me sceptical, but the idea of Oliver, Marc and Owen being solely responsible for getting themselves and four kids wedding-ready makes me nervous. Out of the corner of my eye, I spot Lianna making her way back to the car with more paper bags than she can carry. Quickly saying our goodbyes, I shove my handset into my pocket and rush over to give her a hand.

'Who was on the phone?' She asks, passing me a tray of drinks.

'Oliver.'

'Everything's OK... isn't it?' Her smile momentarily freezes as she rests the mountain of the food on the bonnet of the car.

'Yes! Everything's fine.' I flash her a reassuring smile and dive in for a handful of fries. 'You're the bride. As long as you are OK, everything else will be.'

'Great!' Her cheeks colour up for a second before she shakes off the embarrassment.

'You are OK, aren't you?' I eye up my best friend as the four of us climb back into the car.

'I'm getting married today.' She flashes me a huge smile as she fires up the engine. 'Of course, I am OK.'

As we pull out into the road, I dive into my cheeseburger and watch the world whizz by. Of all of the ways I imagined Lianna would get married, this never crossed my mind. I have to admit that her calmness is unnerving me a little. Has there been a bride in history who has a lie in the morning of her wedding and devours cheeseburgers a few hours before the ceremony? I think not. Looking at her now, her hair blowing in her face as she licks relish from her little finger, I don't think I have ever seen her be more serene and well, happy.

Palm trees fly past the window as Lianna flicks on the radio and signals left. It's hard to believe that she's getting married, today, in a matter of hours. I've never known a wedding like it. Momentarily losing myself in my cheeseburger, I take a huge bite and lean over to steal one of Gina's chips. Batting my hands away, she stuffs the last of her wrap into her mouth as Lianna slams on the brakes. Looking up to see Eve's familiar gates, I let out a laugh as Eve crawls over Li's knee to punch in the passcode.

Straining my neck for a better view, I am surprised to see that everything seems surprisingly calm. There are no children running around, no stressed-out dads losing their cool… it seems a little too good to be true. Unbuckling my seatbelt, I grab the now empty paper bags and slide across the hot leather seat.

'Right, ladies. We have got a *lot* of work to do to get this one bridal ready.' Eve marches off ahead and wags her finger at Lianna. 'No offence.'

'None taken.' Lianna rolls her eyes and links her arm through mine.

'I'm thinking hair first and then we'll do your make-up.' Eve pushes her way inside and drops her bag onto the table with a clatter.

Following her into the villa, I dump my overnight bag and head off in search of Oliver. Thankfully, it doesn't take me long to find them. Tracing the lovely sound of children's laughter, I push open the games room door to find Oliver, Owen, Marc and the kids.

'Oh... You're all dressed.' I bend down to pick up Noah and let out a surprised laugh. 'I am *very* impressed.'

'What did you expect?' Marc asks, holding up Melrose to show off her pretty pink dress.

'To be honest, I thought we might come back to chaos.' Planting a kiss on Oliver's cheek, I smile at Madison as she twirls around for me. 'Well done, guys! You all look fantastic!'

They really do. Madison and Melrose have matching pink ballerina dresses on whilst Noah and MJ look ridiculously cute in their linen trouser suits. Oliver, Owen and Marc are also rocking the laid-back Caribbean look in chinos and short-sleeved shirts. I have to admit that they all look perfect, Madison's hair aside. Not surprisingly for three men, they have resorted to twisting her hair into a messy knot and throwing one too many sparkly clips into the mix.

'Eve will be very happy.' Nodding in approval, I step aside as Eve squeezes in behind me.

'Awwh' Clasping her hands to her heart, she lets out a squeal as MJ jumps into her arms. 'You all look amazing!'

'Let me see!' Gina yells, pushing her way to the front. Wolf whistling loudly, she plucks Melrose from Marc.

'Mummy!' Madison yells, taking a running jump at Gina. 'Look at my dress.'

'Wow! Very pretty!' She whistles as Madison dances around before frowning as she takes in her odd hairstyle. 'Who did your hair, Madison?'

'Me!' She smiles proudly and points to her head.

'That explains it, come with me.' Handing Melrose back to Marc, she takes Madison and leads her into the living room.

'Where's Li?' Oliver asks, straightening out his collar.

'Did someone say my name?' Popping her head around the door, she breaks into a smile as she takes in everyone's outfits.

Owen breaks into a chorus of Here Comes the Bride and it's not long before we all join in. Covering her face with her hands, she blushes a violent shade of purple and lets out an embarrassed cough.

'Has anyone heard from Vernon?' She asks, in a desperate bid to change the subject.

Oliver nods and squeezes her shoulders. 'He's down at The Hangout with his folks. Have you not spoken to him?'

'No, I wanted to keep it traditional.'

'Traditional?' I let out a laugh and bounce Noah on my hip. '*Nothing* about today is traditional.'

Sticking her tongue out, she takes Noah from me and blows a raspberry on his stomach.

'Have you guys eaten?' Owen asks, motioning to the kitchen. 'We have had omelettes, but I thought you might want something more luxurious with it being your wedding day.'

Eve, Lianna and I exchange glances before bursting into hysterics.

'What?' Marc asks, looking at the three of us as though we have lost our minds.

Trying to compose myself, I shake my head and shove the fast food receipt that is hanging out of Lianna's pocket out of sight.

'It's OK. We already ate...'

* * *

This cannot be happening. Tugging at the zip, I pull as hard as I possibly can before looking at Eve and shaking my head.

'It's fine.' Lianna mumbles, sounding totally not bothered. 'I will wear something else.'

'You can't wear something else! This is your wedding dress!' Eve pushes me out of the way and attempts to fasten the zip that is at least two inches away from fitting. 'I *told* you that you should have tried it on!'

Rubbing my throbbing temples, I try to stop the panic that is building in my stomach. We have been trying to get Lianna into her dress for the best part of an hour and I am now more confident than ever that it just isn't going to fit.

'Honestly, I'm... I don't care.' Wiggling out of the too-tight dress, Lianna reaches for a towel and wanders over to the wardrobe.

With her hair beautifully twisted into a classic chignon at the nape of her neck and her makeup totally flawless, she looks so stunningly beautiful. She could walk down the aisle in that very towel and still take everyone's breath away.

Gina bites her nails anxiously and I slap her on the arm. Grubby nails aren't going to help anyone right now. As Eve frantically attempts to magically make the dress a size larger, I look down at my watch and feel my stomach churn. We've got fifteen minutes until we absolutely *have* to leave. Thankfully the boys left with the kids an hour earlier, so all we have to do is get Lianna to The Hangout on time. This sounded so much easier just sixty minutes ago.

'Li?' I whisper, tapping her on the shoulder gently.

Spinning around to face me, she fiddles with her earrings and smiles. 'Yes?'

Pursing my lips, I look at Gina for help. 'What are you looking for?'

'A dress, I guess...' Screwing up her nose, she flicks through the rails and pulls out a beige pencil dress. 'What about this?'

Shaking my head, I start to feel a little sick. What the hell are we going to do? Li is getting married in less than an hour and her dress doesn't bloody fit! It was those damn burgers I know it! Slowly counting to ten to stop myself from having a panic attack, I look down at my beautiful blue gown. We have to get changed, I decide. There's no way we can walk down the aisle like prom queens whilst the bride wears a tight mini dress.

'I've got an idea.' Eve mumbles, holding up the dress. 'What if we put a slash down the other side and we say that it's a cut-out design? You know, like a high-end, risqué, couture...' She trails off into silence as Lianna shakes her head.

'We're not cutting it up.' Li laughs and perches on the end of the bed. 'Honestly, I'm really not bothered. I told you from the start that I didn't care what I wore.'

The most worrying thing of all is that I genuinely believe her. Since she had her first glass of fizz whilst Eve did her hair, all she has talked about is how she can't wait to spend the rest of her life with Vernon. I completely believe that she would marry him in a bin liner.

Grabbing a bottle of bubbles from the dressing table, Eve swigs straight from the bottle and exhales loudly.

'OK. We've got nine minutes.' Pulling Gina and I to one side, she puts on her serious face and hands around the fizz. 'We need to find everything and anything that we have which is white and we need to find it quick...'

* * *

'You look incredible.' Holding a tissue to my eyes, I try and fail to stop the tears from falling.

'Do I really?' A flash of nerves washes across her face as she fiddles with her veil.

Not wanting to risk opening my mouth in case I turn into a blubbering mess, I resort to a swift nod of the head before pulling her in and squeezing her tight. Only Lianna could pull this off. After the most intense ten minutes of my life, we managed to transform Lianna into the most beautiful bride I have ever seen. Anyone else would look ridiculous walking down the aisle in a five-hundred-dollar swimsuit, but somehow, Lianna manages to pull it off perfectly. The striking ice white swimming costume, if you can call it that, is emblazoned with a thousand Swarovski crystals and fits her like a glove. Seriously, it was like it was made for her.

Almost unbelievably, Eve still had some of her honeymoon clothes in the villa and the ridiculously expensive swimwear was handmade by one of her designer friends as a wedding gift. In true Eve fashion, she had a matching kaftan which was just waiting to be worn. The soft, sheer fabric is gathered at the waist in a perfect ribbon, the white silk falling in pleats to the ground. At first, I thought Li had lost her mind when she declared that she would be wearing a swimsuit, but once she had teamed it with the angelic floor-length kaftan, she looks more perfect than I could ever imagine.

Adjusting her veil so that it frames her face perfectly, I hand her the bouquet as the music starts to play.

'I love you.' Squeezing her tightly, I plant a kiss on her cheek and wipe off any remnants of lipstick.

Right on cue, Gina appears through the palm trees with Madison and Melrose.

'They're ready for you!' Smiling brightly, she squeezes Lianna's hand as she lets out a squeal. 'You look stunning, Lianna. Doesn't she look like a princess, Madison?'

Madison looks Lianna up and down for a moment before shaking her head. 'No.' She mumbles, fiddling with her dress.

My jaw drops open as Gina looks down at Madison in horror. 'Madison!'

Throwing herself at Lianna's legs, she wraps her little arms around her and squeezes as hard as she can. 'She doesn't look like a *princess*! She looks like a mermaid. Like the prettiest mermaid in the world.'

Eve and Lianna simultaneously gasp as the music comes to a stop.

'This is it.' I breathe, as the processional music kicks in. 'Are you sure you want to walk down the aisle by yourself? I can get Marc for you?'

'I want to do this on my own.' Shaking her head adamantly, she motions for us to go.

With a final squeeze, I follow Eve and Gina through The Hangout and pause by the hammocks. Around twenty chairs have been decked out in classic white ribbons on either side of the wicker archway that has been positioned in front of the ocean. The sun is starting to set overhead, creating beautiful flashes of red and orange across the sky. Picture perfect, I couldn't have planned it better myself.

As per Lianna's instructions, Madison goes first, remembering to twirl as she goes before coming to a stop and jumping onto Marc's knee. Shuffling forward, I smile at Gina as she takes to the red carpet. With Melrose on her hip, she manages to get to the front without so much as a whimper from the baby. Catching her eye, I offer her a smile as she takes her seat. Eve gives me a nudge before stepping onto the carpet and I watch her strut down the aisle like a pro.

Looking over my shoulder at Lianna, I smile as I notice that she is watching Vernon intently from behind her flowers. With my focus being on the other bridesmaids, I hadn't even looked at Vernon. Standing tall and proud to the right of the archway, smiling like a child on Christmas morning, he looks so happy that I can't help but smile myself. So transfixed by Vernon's smile, I almost miss my cue. Taking a deep breath, I tuck a stray strand of hair behind my ear and step forward, the sea breeze is warm on my skin as I make my way along the carpet, taking in the dozens of smiling faces as I go. Vernon flashes me a wink as I take my seat on the front row and I feel myself on the verge of tears once again.

Reaching over for Oliver's hand, I entwine my fingers with his as the entire wedding party spins around in their seats. The music turns down a notch, the only additional sound coming from the waves as they crash gently against the sand. A few gasps escape people's lips as Lianna makes her way down the aisle. Before I can stop it from happening, tears spill down my cheeks. Big, watery, happy tears fall into my lap and I try desperately to wipe them away.

Pausing halfway down the aisle, Lianna's face breaks into a sparkling smile as she throws down her flowers and takes a running jump into Vernon's arms. The crowd erupts into cheers as Vernon plants a kiss on Lianna's head and squeezes her tightly. Prising them apart, the magistrate laughs loudly and flushes pink.

'Normally the kiss comes *after* the vows...'

Laughter rings around the secluded beach for the second time before falling into silence. An excited buzz hangs in the air as twenty pairs of eyes stare at the happy couple.

'Dearly beloved, we are gathered here today...'

As the magistrate talks animatedly about the amazing commitment of which we are about to witness, I find myself transfixed on the chemistry between Li and Vernon. Not taking their eyes off one another for a second, they seem totally oblivious to the fact that two dozen people are watching their every move. Locking eyes with Oliver, I smile brightly and rest my head on his shoulder as Noah crawls onto my lap.

It's hard to believe that after all of Lianna's dating disasters, after all of the times that she has had her heart broken into a million pieces, her knight in shining armour was waiting for her here all along.

'Love is the dawn of marriage and marriage is the sunset of love…'

Kissing the top of Noah's head, I swallow the lump in my throat as Vernon starts to say his vows. My mother once told me that beginnings are usually scary and endings, well, endings are usually pretty sad, but it's everything in between that makes life worth living. I might not have a crystal ball and I certainly don't know what the future holds for Lianna, but if life has taught me anything, it's that if you love someone you have to set them free.

For no matter how many miles come between my best friend and I, we will always be under the same sky, looking up at the same stars at night. The most beautiful discovery that true friends can make is that they can grow separately without growing apart. Maybe in distance, but never in heart…

To be continued...

The Clara Andrews Series

Meet Clara Andrews
Clara Meets the Parents
Meet Clara Morgan
Clara at Christmas
Meet Baby Morgan
Clara in the Caribbean
Clara in America
Clara in the Middle
Clara's Last Christmas
Clara Bounces Back
Clara's Greek Adventure
Clara and the Billionaire
Clara and the Nanny
Clara's Viva Las Vegas

Have you read the other books by Lacey London?

The Anxiety Girl Series

Anxiety Girl
Anxiety Girl Falls Again
Anxiety Girl Breaks Free

The Mollie McQueen Series

Mollie McQueen is NOT Getting Divorced

Mollie McQueen is NOT Having a Baby

Mollie McQueen is NOT Having Botox

Mollie McQueen is NOT Ruining Christmas

Mollie McQueen is NOT Crashing the Wedding

Follow Lacey London on Twitter

@thelaceylondon

Printed in Great Britain
by Amazon